# Dining with Humboldt Squid

# Dining with Humboldt Squid

### (a Devilly Peen Murder Mystery – #3)

## E.K. Wicher

EKWicherbooks
1400 rue Archambault
Sainte-Adèle
Quebec J8B 2X6
Canada

ISBN 978-1-7774547-6-0 (Paperback)
ISBN 978-1-7774547-7-7 (E-book)

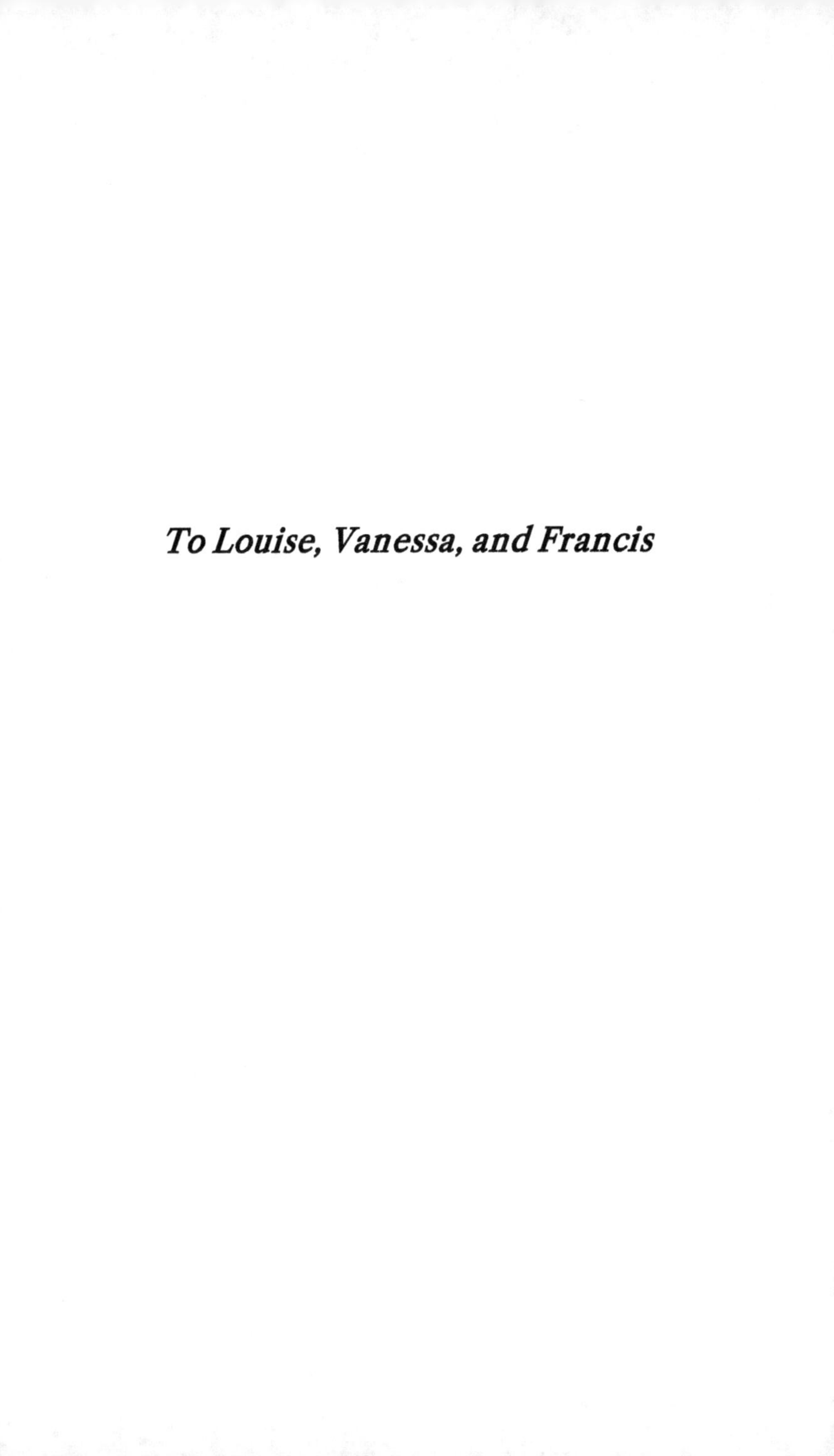

*To Louise, Vanessa, and Francis*

# Glossary

Arboreals—previous inhabitants of Earth, reputed to swing from trees

Blue Peony—a type of showy sea anemone, a cultivar

Black Slug—see nudibranch

Centro—axial city and largest conurbation on the Gyre

Cuttle—cephalopod mollusc; when interbred with octopods considered lower class; a term of disparagement, sometimes of affection

Gyre, the—the vast swirl of plastic in the mid-Pacific colonized by octopods

Holothurian—sea cucumber, tasty but remove the rind

Humboldt Squid—a large squid; an indigenous species known for its ferocity and appetite

Kelpchopper—ground effect vehicle favoured by the emergency services

Octo—the common language of the Pacific Ocean, used by numerous species

Octopod—an eight-armed alien colonist; with the octopus, an example of interplanetary convergent evolution. Also: *octo* (informal)

Plastivorous Worms—annelid worms bio-engineered to eat plastic, a destructive pest

Pulsejet—patrol car

Nether Vortex—a small village on the Gyre, home of Devilly Peen

Nudibranch: *nu.di.brank*—the family of sea slugs, of which the black slugs are the most notorious

Splashdown Day—a celebration of the first arrival of Octopods on Earth, several generations ago

Tetradotoxin—a venom found in various marine species that causes paralysis and death

Tentacle—variously adapted by octopods, comparable to the swiss army knife

# Chapter 1

THE BLUE GLIMMER reflecting from the shop front opposite caught Leo's eye as he was arranging books in the window display. Bling's Books was one of several small independent retailers renting cheap premises in the tottering plastic of the Hipster quarter of Centro. Leo could usually rely on a passing trade of octos wafting towards the theatre district and pausing to browse, but it had been a quiet afternoon with few customers. Now a police vehicle was plugging the narrow passage that separated Leo's shop from the tattoo parlor opposite. That should scare away whoever might be left of his reading public, he thought.

An octo officer pushed aside the drape of weed, and entered the shop, flashing three stripes on several of his thick arms. He was followed into the shop by a willowy octopod in plain clothes.

"Oleaginous Bling?"

"The same," answered Leo. "How may I help you, Officer?"

"I am Sergeant Pulper from Centro Police. We are looking for a book: *Serial Suckers* by Devilly Peen."

Leo nodded to the display.

"Devilly will be here for a signing tomorrow, if you would like to come back. But if you buy one now, they are discounted twenty percent for the launch."

The Sergeant picked up a copy and looked curiously at the cover. He passed it to his companion who rapidly flicked through the pages, gazing intently, before nodding.

"Is this the lot?" asked Pulper. "Or do you have others in the back?"

"I think, yes, that is all fifty copies." Leo hesitated, puzzled by the question.

"We'll take them all."

"Whoa! You don't want them gift wrapped, I hope? That might take a while."

"No, we have a sack. Oh, and we won't be buying: these books are proceeds of crime and are evidence."

# Chapter 2

THE RED LIGHT began to blink, warning Devilly that the tape was full. Never mind: her secretary could finish the sentence. If it wasn't obvious by now whodunnit, frankly then the reader should stick with romcoms. The new machine that allowed her to dictate her books made life so much easier. She could hardly remember how she had managed without it—tapping away on the old Remington, tentacles flying.

"Annie?" she called from her study. "I have another tape for you. It is the last for this one. After you type it up, let WordscribblerXT have a go at it. We might as well make the most of the one-month free promotion. Then, I think we'll take a break. Our publisher should be happy: we are ages before the deadline."

Anemone Pilchard and her sister Sylphy had been in Devilly's employ for several months.

They were of the same brood and looked identical. Devilly—desperate for staff and accepting applicants from an agency recommended by her friend Margo Seethe-Mantle—employed both. One did Devilly's typing and paperwork; the other cooked, cleaned and looked after the garden. Although a simple division of responsibilities, Devilly could never be sure which twin was which. She suspected that they swapped tasks, sixteen tentacles being better than eight.

Now, duty done, and writing finished for the day, Devilly could prepare for the visit of her friend from the city. Anna Teuthis—Doctor Teuthis—was a consulting pathologist in Centro and rented one of the grottages just up from Devilly. It was a small *pied a terre*, and certainly not as pleasant as Devilly's Rose Grottage. A weekender, yes, but Anna was happy to adapt to village ways. The upcoming weekend was a special outing of the Nether Vortex Ramblers, a group of walkers and nature lovers, and Devilly had little trouble in persuading Anna to come along.

Usually, the club excursions were local, exploring tortuous routes through the bottle fields that lay round about, taking in sites of particular interest such as Ariadne's Web, a tangle of fishing floats with nets attached, or exploring the few nearby patches of plastic jungle that had escaped the ravages of development. If truth be told, Devilly had begun to find these excursions a little repetitive. Numbers had dropped off lately; the ramblers who turned out on weekends had dwindled to three.

It was Devilly's secretary who had suggested visiting the White Islands Sanctuary. It was the largest wilderness area on the outer Gyre, she had explained enthusiastically, with miles of trails, wild swimming, and a sublime coastline. It would be a perfect outing for the Ramblers. And, they could stay at a country inn she knew just outside the borders of the Sanctuary. By great good luck, that very morning Anemone had extricated a brochure from the junk floating in their mail pool.

"It's called *Bottlings*, and I think they have a website." Anenome had stayed there two years previously and had found the the accommodation charmingly rustic, with the food good and freshly plucked from the ocean.

So, when Devilly happened to bump in to Margo Seethe-Mantle in the coffee shop in Nether Vortex, she mentioned the White Islands Sanctuary as the perfect spot for an outing of the Ramblers, and produced the brochure for *Bottlings*.

Margo, who had also come to find the Ramblers' recent excursions rather tame, agreed wholeheartedly that the Sanctuary would be perfect.

"But where else can we stay?" she added dubiously. "Just look at those room prices."

"They seem reasonable to me, for a 3 star," said Devilly, remembering that the Seethe-Mantles, for all their aristocratic pretensions, were rich in plastic but cash poor. To be honest, they were cheap when it came to parting with the ready.

"There must be something cheaper in the area." Margo consulting her smart phone. "There, I thought so. The White Islands Campground is actually inside the Sanctuary. That will be perfect."

She showed the phone to Devilly: the

campground looked decent, and much cheaper than staying at *Bubblings*. But luckily—from Devilly's point of view—the campground was closed for the season—responding to conservation priorities, apparently.

"So, it looks like the country inn is the only option," said Devilly. "And it has a pool."

"Well, all right. I suppose you should book it. Roger will be disappointed—he is a keen camper, you know."

Devilly guessed that Roger would be only too happy not to camp—sharing a tent with Margo might be a change from their rambling warren of a manor house, but Roger was not one to embrace change. Especially if fresh seas gave his wife an appetite.

"I'll go ahead and ask Anemone to book the rooms. I'm bringing my friend Anna Teuthis. She will be down from the city and is keen to join us."

"Well, of course. If she is a friend of yours, I am sure she will be good value."

Devilly suddenly remembered that the Seethe-Mantles were a little stiff with second homeowners who only appeared in Nether

Vortex on weekends.

"Shouldn't we ask Colonel Seethe-Mantle about the trip?" asked Devilly, knowing the question would annoy Margo. Margo's snort of amusement at the thought of her husband's possible dissent came as no surprise.

✧　✧　✧

LATER THAT AFTERNOON, on the way back to Rose Grottage, Devilly popped into the Nether Vortex library and asked whether they had anything on the White Islands Sanctuary. She left with an illustrated travel book that listed the sanctuary as number eight on a must-do list for Gyre nature lovers. The nearby seaside village of Crabster was noted as picturesque, with good seafood. The area was famous for birdwatching.

Anna was a real enthusiast and kept a check list of birds she had spotted across the Gyre. She told Devilly that her hobby was the antidote to her job as forensic pathologist in the city morgue. Anna was especially keen to visit the Sanctuary where several rare species were recently spotted. Scenes of violent crime, Anna had explained, only attract the ruder gulls; other birds tend to shun their company.

Devilly did not want to appear ignorant. She spent the evening thumbing through her dog-eared field guide to Birds of the Gyre and dug out an old pair of binoculars.

And it would not just be birds—there was plenty of other wildlife to see. From the guide she gathered they could hike out along the coast to the extremity of the Gyre, where they might see a spawning, when gravid fish rose from the mid-levels to the surface and engaged in riotous procreation. Or, being next to the open ocean, they might see whales.

"I'm going to meet my friend at the station now," called Devilly into the kitchen, as she swung open the clam shell front door. "Just a simple supper will do, Sylphy—one never has much appetite after the tiresome suck of the pneumatic."

A faint acknowledgment came from the rear of the grottage. Either of the twins, she couldn't be sure.

It was true, thought Devilly, that the pneumatic network of plastic tubes that now extended to Nether Vortex could shoot you up to town and back in no time. However, the pressure differences always left her with a migraine and barely able to face even a crab sandwich.

Anna's pneumatic arrived on schedule, the tube dismissing its sole passenger with a farewell hiss as the pressures equalized.

"Anna! Over here!" Devilly waved in welcome.

Anna glided down the platform, trailing a rucksack by one tentacle. She embraced Devilly with several of her other arms.

"I really didn't think I would be able to get away. The morgue was beginning to fill up— the usual Friday night crowd . . . but the help has to learn . . . gosh, you look well!"

"Oh, well, thank you. It is a wonder you could come, but I'm really pleased. The trip tomorrow is going to be much more fun. Otherwise, it would be just me and the Seethe-Mantles—Margo is great fun but, you know . . ."

The two friends left the station and jetted swiftly along the main channel through the village, before turning down the wetlane towards the grottages. They reached Anna's weekend place first.

"I'll just pop in and see if everything is all right."

"Well, don't be long. Then come down to Rose Grottage. I asked Sylphy to put together a light meal, or we could catch something out in the garden."

"It will have to be an early night, though. Otherwise, I'll be a total wreck tomorrow."

✧ ✧ ✧

ROGER SEETHE-MANTLE HAD volunteered to drive, grumbling but ever under the orders of Margo. Next morning found the Ramblers piling into the estate SeaRover, a suitably battered country transport. With four octopods and their suitcases, plus Devilly's portable typewriter—she never went anywhere without it—meant that Anna and Devilly had to squeeze in the back. Margo took the front seat beside her husband.

After a few false starts, they found themselves a likely route leading through the swirling plastic in the direction of the outer Gyre. Routes changed frequently at the whim of the currents, and Roger had printed out the latest maps. But Margo chose to ignore these, preferring to relay instructions from her phone app.

"Left at the next junction," she insisted, and it was only when it became apparent that veering right was the only sensible option, that she allowed Roger to continue. Left was blocked by an impassable sludge of plastic bags.

"Only another half an hour," called Margo over her shoulder to the rear passengers who were beginning to suffer *mal de mer* from the frequent twists and turns.

"You would think," muttered Devilly to her co-sufferer, "that they would have stabilized these channels by now. It is one of the main routes to this outer arm from Centro ... oh no!"

The SeaRover had come up behind another vehicle, a camper advancing by slow suck and pull. It was the kind to make any driver groan:

too wide to pass easily, and apt to accelerate whenever a potential passing opportunity arose. Roger slammed his tentacle against the steering wheel in frustration. They had been gliding along at a good clip but now their speed reduced to a crawl.

"We'll be stuck behind this thing forever, damn it," grumbled Roger. "Pull over, won't you!"

"Patience, darling," said Margo, looking up from her app.

Roger wound two arms around the wheel and squeezed hard with his suckers. Devilly thought the colour of the back of his neck alarming.

"Margo, would you . . ." he began, but then the camper slowed, pulled to the side and an arm waved them on. The SeaRover accelerated smoothly past.

"Bloody decent of him," muttered Roger, pressing on.

The tube that opened before them was empty of traffic. The plastic became increasingly rustic, heavy with weed and dripping with barnacles; they were leaving the cultivated fields behind and entering a wilder country. Devilly could taste the change in the water, and a distinct swell began to lift and let fall the tube before them.

"All right back there?" called Roger. "Only another half hour."

✧  ✧  ✧

"I WANTED TO tell you how grateful I am for the invitation."

Anna was leaning towards Devilly and whispering in her ear.

"What? Oh, of course, you are always welcome."

"No, I mean it. Things have been a bit stressful back in town. I really needed to get away."

"Why, have the corpses been piling up?"

"No, it's not work. I have been getting death threats."

"What?"

"Death threats. You know that anti-abortion mob that are always demonstrating in Centro, picketing the family help clinics and generally making themselves obnoxious. Well, somehow they found out about my terminations. I keep getting these reminders in my mail. *One in a Thousand* they call themselves. I throw them away."

"That is harassment. No one today can be expected to carry a thousand eggs, starve for six months and then die. It's a hark-back to the Middle Ages."

"Yes, you think that, and I think that, but there is this idea that natural reproduction—raw and bloody as it may be—is always best. They think me a murderer."

"How dreadful for you. And, statistically speaking, only two of the thousand would survive in the wild anyway. Have you talked to the police?"

"I doubt that would do much good. The police are helpless in these situations."

"Have you told your exes, at least. They must have endorsed the procedure."

"Well, as you know Devilly, I don't get on well with either of them."

No, I can imagine, thought Devilly. The problem with a tri-sexual species like octopods was that there was a perpetual triangle of parental interest. Theoretically, this encouraged responsible parenthood, but times change, and what had been a solid social commitment had become a licence for promiscuity. Or so it seemed from observation—Devilly herself never having experimented with that particular geometry of relationships; she had, in her younger days, been happy enough with mail order.

"I suppose you will just have to ignore it. Surely it is nothing but nastiness. Anyway, you can forget all about it for the weekend. After this journey and Roger's driving, they will never find you."

"Oh Devilly, you are right as usual. I shall concentrate on the birds and to hell with the trolls. Heh! Didn't we just pass a sign? We must be almost there."

Roger backed up and they turned to follow the arrow to the White Islands Sanctuary. As they drove, the way narrowed to a thin neck with deep blue ocean on either side. Ahead, a high mound of floating garbage crowned by old growth plastic lifted and fell on the swells, and, far in the distance, Devilly had her first sight of the White Islands rising from the sea mist as a magnificent backdrop. What a view!

They came to a fork: turn left for White Islands; right for the village of Crabster. They turned left, passed through a gate and entered the Sanctuary. Roger pulled into the Visitor Centre and turned off the engine.

"Made it," he said. "Now that wasn't so bad, was it?"

# Chapter 3

THE HIDE WAS of sturdy construction: a tough but transparent plastic that could—if the need arose—repel the dive-bombing of the most aggressive gannet. Now though, in late afternoon, the returning seabirds were tired, their gorges replete from scouring the surrounding ocean of fish. Intent on feeding their chicks and reclaiming their spots on the island for their night roost, they chose to ignore the huddled group of octopods beneath their plastic shield.

Through thin slits just above the water surface, the watchers trained their binoculars on the snow-white peak across the narrow channel. This, perhaps the loftiest of several similar islands around the extreme periphery of the Gyre, had been recently designated the White Islands Sanctuary, a protected area for wildfowl. Established to preserve the nesting sites of avian species who had adopted this giant raft of plastic waste in the open ocean, the site was a favoured destination for "twitchers".

Devilly shared the hide with Anna and the two other members of the Nether Vortex Ramblers, each keen to get the best view. Despite retaining in her arms a bundle of floats, to keep her head above water, Devilly was frequently jostled by her neighbour, which made it difficult to focus on the distant birds.

"It's all in the breathing," muttered Roger Seethe-Mantle to Devilly, after he had nudged her for the third time. "Take your time, breathe in and out, and then focus."

"There are just too many arms and tentacles in this confined space," grumbled Devilly, while trying to keep her binoculars trained on the swirling clouds of seabirds.

"Behave yourself, Roger," admonished his wife Margo from the Colonel's other side. All the Ramblers had opted for a tweedy colour scheme, so it was admittedly difficult to determine whose arm belonged to whom.

Crouched at the rear of the hide, their

guide—a young octopod on a gap year—was keen to ensure that his group benefited from the educational materials developed by the Sanctuary.

"We are a joint project of the regional council and the central government," he announced to their backs, causing them all to start. "First discovered on the outer Gyre thirty revolutions ago, the original colony comprised only twelve birds. These clung to an isolated clump of plastic waste bound by ribbons of cling film. With the passage of time, the birds' ejecta cemented the plastic into a sturdy platform, and what we now know as the White Islands began to grow."

"*Ejecta?*" asked Devilly, always with a keen author's ear for usage.

"Er, I mean, bird poo," acknowledged their guide, flushing pink to tentacle tip. "Ahem. Now the island is home to many thousands of nesting pairs."

"I have ocean guillemots," whispered Anna. "And just to the left is a whole group of boobies."

"Look! Is that an albatross coming in to

land?" Devilly looked down at the illustrated guide she had picked up at the Visitor's Centre. "It might be the lesser, judging by the markings."

"No, Devilly: that is just another gull," corrected Anna. "You would never see an albatross in this company."

The sun burst through the patchy clouds to shine obliquely on the island, causing Devilly's pupils to narrow in the brilliant light. It was, she knew, reflecting from the pure white nitrate that had been deposited by generations of birds. An acrid smell reached them across the water; the White Islands were literally breath-taking. It had been well-worth the long trip from Nether Vortex.

"And of course, there is an important economic consideration," resumed their guide, after glancing quickly at his notes. "The *ejecta* erodes under the action of wind and waves and forms a plume of nutrient-rich particles in the waters beneath the island. This plume nourishes a rich diversity of plankton which in turn serves to feed the many fish farms down current. Once again, environmental responsibility is serving the needs of our pisciculturalists, and our growing octopod population."

Thereby fulfilling several election promises of the current government, thought Devilly, a little jadedly, as she recalled the ever-rising price of fish.

# Chapter 4

THE LONG JET back to the Visitor Centre at White Islands Sanctuary sapped the last of the energy from Nether Vortex Ramblers. They were an elderly group, after all, and it had been a full day. After the morning drive from Nether Vortex and a hasty lunch *al fresco*, they had been in the field all afternoon; exciting but exhausting. Now, after saying goodbye to their guide, they looked forward to a relaxing evening.

The Ramblers climbed thankfully into the SeaRover.

"Let's just have a look at the campsite for next time," said Margo. "I saw the sign on the way in."

It was a short detour to the designated area. Roger pulled up, and they all gazed at the desolate patch of windblown sea strewn with trash. "No campers", said a sign.

A lucky escape, thought Devilly.

✧　✧　✧

LEAVING THE SANCTUARY, they turned towards the village of Crabster. They began to see new construction beside their route: rows of bottle condos were going up. "Sea and Sanctuary", proclaimed one large billboard; "Just imagine!", another, with a picture of a grinning octopod family.

"I've seen the promotions." commented Margo, as they went past. "They are all built with organic yogurt pots, and are selling as one, two or three-pot plans. Outrageously expensive."

A little further on, set back from the road, a mansion was under construction. Black plastic siding and windows featured prominently. Contractors were milling about, looking busy.

"I wonder who that belongs to," wondered Devilly. "It must have a fine view of the sea."

"Some idiot out of Centro with more money than sense," said Roger. "They are taking over the countryside."

The old part of Crabster consisted of a single street along the waterfront, a charming if eclectic mishmash of plastic containers of all sorts and sizes. Most of the shops seemed to sell beach ware.

A little beyond the village, past sea meadows sprinkled with colourful bottle caps, they finally arrived at *Bottlings*. The Inn huddled at the end of a narrow splinter of sea where windrows of purple plastic rose *en echelon* from a carpet of creamy foam, a sight that would normally elicit cries of delight from visitors.

"God, I need a drink," said Margo.

*Bottlings* promised cozy accommodation. Once a run-down country pub, it now boasted a restaurant—apparently the only place to eat for miles. Meals were served in the lounge bar, or, when the water was warmer, outside in the anemone garden. A packed lunch could be provided on request for its clientele of outdoorsy types. It had a 3-star rating.

The lady octopod overflowing a cranny behind Reception was effusive in her welcome.

"Oh, my dears, you look frozen stiff. Have

you been out there on the White Islands all day?"

"Well, yes," replied Devilly, acting as spokesperson for the group. "We have reservations for this evening: for Peen, Seethe-Mantle and Teuthis. I am Devilly Peen."

"Welcome to *Bottlings*. I'm Mrs. Blackpen, but please call me Cephy. Let me just check . . . ah yes, Ms. Peen: we have you and Ms. Teuthis in Magnum. It's a nice double room with portholes looking out towards the ocean . . ."

"But we asked for two singles," insisted Devilly.

Mrs. Blackpen paused and looked first at Devilly and then at Anna.

"My mistake. Of course, dear. We can put you in *Beaujolais*, and Ms. Teuthis in *Bordeaux:* two single rooms—*uno litro*, as the French say. Your rooms are in the Annex.

"The Annex?" asked Devilly.

"Yes, the Magnum you reserved is here in the main building, but we are almost full. We've never seen such a rush at this time of year. Even our Jeroboam Suite is booked for the week. No room at the Inn, ha ha. But the

Annex is very nice and private. It is through the garden, and right beside the pool."

"That sounds nice," said Devilly.

"Right then, that's settled. Now," continued Mrs. Blackpen, "Mr. and Mrs. Mantle, you had a double—but now we can move you to our Magnum, here in the main building."

"It's Colonel and Mrs. Seethe-Mantle," corrected Roger, stiffening.

"Well, to be sure." Cephy held out several pens with her tentacles. "Please sign in."

There followed the usual confusion of arms as the octopods tried to write at the same time.

"I hope you saw the birds you wanted," said Cephy, as she prepared the room keys. "My Hubby says birds is all very well, but they do make a mess. Did you make reservations for dinner? Kitchen closes at 8."

"Where is the restaurant?" asked Margo.

"Our Bubbles Lounge and Restaurant is here on the left, and we have the Public Bar through the tunnel on the right."

"And what is in here?" Devilly was peering through an opening opposite the entrance to the lounge. On the far wall, a weed-draped piano looked as though it hadn't been played for ages.

"That is the drawing room. It is for guests only. We have games and magazines. My Hubby, Mr. Blackpen, says it has the best view of all our rooms."

As soon as they had all registered, Margo and Roger edged towards the entrance to the bar, but Devilly and Anna made their excuses.

"We are exhausted and simply must lie down. We'll meet you later for supper."

⁂ ⁂ ⁂

THE ANNEX WAS reached by swimming around the side of the main structure, and through a low maintenance garden of plastic beads and dead or dying barnacles. In the midst of the garden was a dark hollow, fenced around, with a sign informing them that the "Blue Lagoon" was closed for maintenance. Circumventing the fencing, Devilly and Anna arrived at their destination, a row of half-shells labeled as French wine regions.

"Thank Goodness, here is *Beaujolais*," cried

Devilly. "I don't care if the bottle *was* found in the flotsam, I am exhausted!"

"Me too," replied Anna, fiddling with the reluctant key pass of *Bordeaux* next door. "But they say they have a hot tub somewhere. I'm going for a soak."

Devilly pushed open the door to *Beaujolais*, and found a modest grotto, sparingly decorated, with much of the space taken up by the sleeping bottle itself. She squeezed inside and flopped, gazing vaguely at a print of dead starfish on the opposite wall.

Devilly woke with a start nearly half an hour later and looked at the time. She had been fast asleep. And she had promised to meet Anna in the Bubbles Lounge ten minutes ago.

After a quick change from birding camouflage into something more appropriate, Devilly hurried back to the Inn. There was no sign of Anna in the foyer, so Devilly wafted under the arch that led into the Lounge and looked around. She was immediately struck by the colour scheme, overwhelmingly in shades of pink and cream. Plastic mouldings of giant clams were grouped artfully for ease of conversation; nooks overstuffed with puff plastic into which one could withdraw discreetly ran around the walls. In all, there was an excess of bubble wrap for Devilly's taste. It was a style she had heard described witheringly by Margo as Gastro-kitsch.

A glance at the wall hangings confirmed that the nearby Sanctuary was clearly the main local attraction: art photographs of birds decorated the walls beside amateur renderings in acrylics of the White Islands on a limpid sea, glimpsed through mist, or rising above storm-whipped spume. Each carried a discreet price tag. Above the faux fireplace floated a chain of illuminated plastic ducks—common enough finds, she supposed, around the margins of the Gyre. They cast a pale light.

A bar occupied one corner of the lounge, supervised by a large octopod of florid com-plexion. By the proprietary way he/she was monitoring the till, Devilly guessed this to be their landlord: "Hubby" she thought. As Devilly approached, his tentacles looped across the spigots that controlled the selection of drinks on tap.

"A good evening, madam. I'm Mr. Blackpen; you will have already met the Ladywife? Good, good. Now, what is our drinking pleasure?" He gestured to the row of real bottles on the glass shelf behind him. Backed by mirrors, they glimmered tantalizingly in the mood lighting.

"Do you serve tea?" inquired Devilly.

"Tea? Yes, we have some somewhere." He reached below the bar and retrieved a tub of sachets. "The Ladywife is the expert, but our house brand is very popular with our guests."

"Oh, all right. For two please."

The landlord selected two sachets and slotted them into a shiny infuser standing on the corner of the bar.

"Thirty seconds," he said. "These new machines are such time savers."

"Oh, yes?" said Devilly, who had never progressed past the simple teapot.

"And from what part of the Gyre are we visiting from?"

"Nether Vortex. You have probably never heard of it."

"Of course, of course. That is a nice bit of country down there. The Ladywife has a cousin in Vortice Main. We visited once, but it is hard to get away from all this." The Landlord swung an all-embracing tentacle, narrowly missing the bottles behind him.

"Yes, Vortice Main is our county town. It is only a short ride from our village."

During the subsequent pause in conversation the infuser began to bubble. Nearly ready. Devilly felt she should make an effort. "Did you take those photographs?"

"No. Chap in the village. Arty type."

Friend of the Ladywife, thought Devilly.

"Are we with the bird group, then? Here to see the mountain, are we? It is a quiet time of year for us, although we had a group up from Centro all week. They left yesterday."

"Naturalists?"

"No, a corporate group took one of our grottage lets for team building. Bunch of yobs; I had to send a rush order for more bottles. Now it is just you, and a professor from the university and his assistant. And then there is the passing trade." He nodded towards a family in the corner and lowered his voice. "They stop for breakfast in their camper vans. I should charge them a fee to use our facilities."

"We think the tea must be ready," said Devilly, wondering why Mrs. Blackpen had relegated Anna and herself to the Annex if trade was as slack as her husband described.

"What? Oh, of course." The landlord filled two syringes with brown fluid and passed them to Devilly.

Retiring to one of the clam mouldings, Devilly sipped her tea. She realized that she was now alone in the lounge bar. The family who had been seated near the fireplace had slipped away, seemingly through the door marked Ladies, Gents and Others, leaving behind the remains of crab-in-a-basket which was already attracting clean-up shrimp. The flames that had danced on the screen before the faux fireplace had switched to the faux aquarium; an illusion of warmth replaced by a real chill.

After serving her, the landlord had disappeared through the partition signed Public Bar from which emanated the drone of animated conversation. A livelier lot than in here, thought Devilly.

She heard a loud laugh and realized that

Margo and Roger had slipped into the Public. Devilly guessed that Roger was regaling the locals with one of his jokes. She recognized Margo's voice; it confirmed her suspicion that the Seethe-Mantles might be avoiding her company.

✧   ✧   ✧

"THERE YOU ARE!" With some relief, Devilly turned towards Anna, who had appeared in the doorway to the lounge, still flushed from the hot tub.

"Is that tea for me; you are a life saver!"

Anna joined Devilly in the clam shell and sucked appreciatively.

"By the way, I enjoyed your last book, *Pretty in Gelatin*. Quite a coincidence, wasn't it?"

"What was?"

"Well, that octo you dispatched in the last chapter. Name of Ordo Whitecuttle—I had him on my slab this week."

"What on earth do you mean?"

"Same description: middle-aged male octo,

overweight. My guy had even expired from multiple knife thrusts, just as in your novel, but he was living on borrowed time anyway. Iffy liver."

Devilly was silent, shocked. One always did a search on names to make sure that one's character did not correspond to a real person. And one always put a disclaimer in the front matter to discourage an angry lawsuit.

"It is almost as though you were clairvoyant," continued Anna. "I hope you don't send anymore my way!"

Now, Devilly's knowledge of the technical aspects of forensic science came from Anna. Her friend was one of the leading pathologists on the Gyre, and on several occasions had been persuaded to talk about the details of some particularly gruesome autopsy, usually over a bottle of wine. Some elements, she consciously included in her writing, but perhaps subconsciously? Devilly had assumed this was a one-way communication.

"But that is not possible. I was sure my name for that character was original."

"*Whitecuttle* is hardly original. The phone

book must have dozens."

Devilly felt slightly dizzy. She didn't recall using that name in her novel: surely, she wouldn't have made such an elementary mistake?"

"Are you all right?" Anna leaned over, looking concerned.

No, she was not all right, but at that moment the door to the public swung open and Margo and Roger emerged and came somewhat unsteadily towards their table.

"We were looking for you two," said Roger. "Let's see if we can order some food."

# Chapter 5

NEXT MORNING, DAPPLED sunlight slanting through the glass walls of *Beaujolais* woke Devilly. Her bottle was only 750 millilitres, but she had squeezed in through the narrow neck without much trouble, one arm at a time, and spent the night in snug comfort. At home, she had a more commodious roost, but she supposed one had to make do in these country inns, 3 stars or not.

After Anna's insistence, Devilly had tried the hot tub before going to bed. It seemed to have worked its wonders—she was only slightly stiff from the exertions of the previous day. The Lord knows what she might have caught from the steaming water—kept at a temperature perfect for incubating pathogens—but so far, so good.

The Ramblers convened in the lounge for breakfast where the alluring tastes of the open ocean washing in through the open windows, mingled with the fishy aromas of breakfast. It was a bracing combination.

"Going hiking this morning, are we?" Mr. Blackpen was serving breakfast in the lounge—today it was kipper on damp toast. "It'll be a good day for it, I reckon. Overcast with light rain is perfect for us fish, as they say. But you can never trust the weather around here. Might turn out brilliant sunshine."

"What's this about a hunt?" asked Roger, who had been scrutinizing the fliers in Reception.

"Ah, that'll be the Humboldt. You are in luck; there is is a meet here today. You'll see them swirling about outside in a few minutes before they set off."

"Isn't it supposed to be a re-enactment of the hunts that the Arboreals used to amuse themselves with?"

"Yes: chasing and killing foxes, whatever they were. Brings me some business, what with the tourists and the protesters, but they are more trouble than they are worth, in my humble opinion. The hunt is just a bunch of stuck-ups, I don't mind telling you. Just 'cos they're rich, they think they own the place."

"Protesters?" asked Devilly.

"Aye, I had a bunch in the Public last night. Rowdy crowd: students. They turn up at every hunt and wave placards. Much good that does. Still, all that protesting gives them a thirst, I'm happy to say."

"Well, if they are going after vermin, I should say a hunt is a good thing," replied Colonel Seethe-Mantle. He kept a small herd of holothurians to graze the algal growth on the plastic around the hobby farm. Lately, he had been having trouble with a squat lobster who seemed partial to sea cucumbers.

"Porpoise."

"What, they hunt porpoises!" exclaimed Anna and Devilly simultaneously. Although neither had seen a porpoise in the wild—being familiar only with the raw *muktuk* on the menu in the fancier restaurants in Centro—they *had* watched programs on television lauding the intelligence of the beasts.

"They are only fish," interjected Margo. "I don't know what all the fuss is about."

"Porpoises are mammals, Margo, and almost as intelligent as the lower classes of octopus," said Devilly firmly. "I'm with the protesters—killing them is almost murder."

To preempt further debate on the pros and cons of the hunt, Roger unfolded a map and spread it between two tentacles.

"This is the recommended route. Starting here in the car park of *Bottlings*, it takes us to the very end of this spiral. The Guide says quote 'the views of the open ocean are unsurpassed' unquote."

"How long is the swim?" asked Anna, dubiously.

"If we leave after breakfast, we should get there by noon. Shall we meet in, say, ten minutes?" He glanced outside. "Oh ho, I see things are already warming up. The hunt is arriving."

They crowded at the front window to look out on a froth of lashing tentacles, as a group of scarlet octos were attempting to climb aboard uncooperative squid.

"Aye, toffs," commented the landlord. "Yonder is Sir Callas Bling. Calls himself Master of Squid. Fancies himself he does, in all that pink and gold. Never more bling than Bling, we say around here."

The Master was berating a group of hunt protesters whose placards were annoying the squid, his colours becoming more saturated by the minute. He had the advantage of riding a particularly aggressive squid who tried to bite one of the students. A "Save the Porpoise" sign floated past.

"Well, perhaps we should wait until the hubbub has died down before trying to leave," said Devilly.

✧   ✧   ✧

A SHORT TIME later, the hunt departed, trailed at some distance by the protesters. The Ramblers gathered outside in the courtyard of the Inn.

"Shall we?" said Roger.

They set off, ready to work off the effects of their leisurely breakfasts. They had modified their skin colours to the mottled blue and grey of the non-biodegradable plastic that lay about them—a suitably rustic camouflage.

Initial signage to the Promontory Trail from the car park beside the Inn was clear and the Ramblers followed the way markers placed by the Gyre Rambling Association. The morning was cool, and they slipped briskly through the twisting channel that led out towards "Land's End."

Their route bordered the splinter of ocean leading from the Inn towards the open sea. The flotsam here was neatly aligned in parallel ridges—formed by successive rafts of plastic straws blowing in from the west. These formed a low barrier between them and the open water, a synthetic barrier reef. The going was easy: they followed the grain of the plastic, slipping readily along just below the water surface. Sometimes, their route tunneled through pressure ridges—formed by the plastic mass buckling under stress. Here and there, they were obliged to swim short distances in open water before regaining the shelter of the barrier. The further they went, the more intermittent the signage, and it was easy to get lost in the bifurcating tunnels. However, they could rely on the obvious wear to the walls of the main route. The group that preceded them had been careless with litter, and they came across evidence of their recent passage: discarded drink sachets and cling-film wrappings.

"You would think those environmentalists would be careful about litter," said Margo.

The tunnel they were following suddenly narrowed as it bored through a massive barrier of plastic bottles. The Ramblers were forced to drop back into single file behind Margo, who was leading.

Devilly had read that these tunnels were the work of plastivorous worms—an invasive species, genetically modified by the Arboreals in a desperate attempt to reduce plastic pollution. For years the worms had run riot in the Gyre, their destructive burrowings causing significant property damage. Now regularly culled, outbreaks were rare. One positive aspect of the worms' ravages was the creation of a network of borings that laced through the Gyre. Many of these had been repurposed for recreational purposes, being charmingly unconstrained by the hub-and-spoke planning model imposed by central government.

At an arrow pointing to their destination, Margo turned into a secondary tunnel that rose gently upwards. "This might be a tight squeeze," she called back, inserting first one tentacle and then another before she slimming to a pencil shape and disappearing with a faint plop. The other Ramblers followed, Devilly glad that she had done her stretches that morning.

The tunnel twisted upwards until emerging above the water level into the open air. Finally, a view of the ocean! The group found themselves at the edge of a ragged cliff formed by a thick raft of floating plastic. It bobbed up and down. They had arrived at The Promontory: a commanding reef of plastic that bulged several tentacles above the sea surface, an altitude seldom reached in the surrounding country.

The Ramblers were in the open air now, and Devilly breathed deeply of the salty air, thankful for her amphibious constitution. The Ramblers gathered at the edge, gazing out at the open ocean. The view was breathtaking, but, beneath them the reef was so riddled with worm tunnels that it seemed like a fragile sponge. Thankfully, it was stabilized by masses of clinging mussels. Looking down into the water, Devilly spotted the waving arms of a giant anemone with its attendant clown.

"Look there!" She pointed out the little, orange-striped fish to Anna.

"Oh, how cute."

A long swell rolled towards and under them, the wave unbroken against this forgiving shore. The water was the dark blue of the deep ocean, the surface smooth as silk. But, far on the horizon, a line of dark clouds suggested approaching weather.

Which reminded Devilly that she should renew her sunscreen. She was comfortable above water provided she kept her skin moist.

"Anna, do you have sun block in your mantle? I'm afraid I forgot mine at the Inn."

"Here," said Anna, passing the tube. "Hey, are those our hunt protesters over there?" She pointed along the edge of the cliff to where a group of octos had gathered. All were gazing intently out to sea.

"What are they looking at? I can't see any-thing."

Devilly pointed to a patch of agitated water some distance from shore.

"It's the hunt!" cried Roger. "We are going to have a front row seat!"

Now they could make out the silver flashes of fish as they leapt from the churning sea, desperate to escape some circling predator. Anticipating a massacre, birds hovered over-head. A trumpet note sounded from across the water; a Neptune's trumpeting—a rallying cry, taken up and echoed by the mewing gulls.

"There!"

Red shapes rose from the waves in bursts of spray before sinking back below water. They encircled the school of fish like a ruby necklace strangling a victim's neck. Through their binoculars they could make out scarlet octos, clinging—it seemed for dear life—to the backs of the Humboldts, those ferocious squid that Devilly knew could hardly be considered civilized. It was becoming a maelstrom of slaughter.

"It all seems a little barbaric," muttered Anna in Devilly's ear.

One of the hunters peeled off from the chase and swam slowly towards them.

"Damn squid threw me," shouted the octo.

"Looks like you have had a bit of luck, finding that school of fish," called Roger.

"No. It's the squid. They catch the scent of mackerel and its impossible to rein them in."

"So, no porpoise, today?"

By now the octo had swum up to them and was clinging to the edge of the plastic below them. His bright pink skin faded to purple.

"There's never any bloody porpoise. Those damn protesters see to that, what with all their noise. I hope you're not with that lot." He waved an arm towards the group of protesters. "Mind you, it is good exercise anyway, but these Humboldts are the devil to ride. Here, help me up."

Roger reached down and hauled the tired hunter from the sea.

"Thanks. Name is McKraken. Are you all staying at *Bottlings*?"

Roger grunted an affirmative and did the honours.

"It must be very exciting, riding a squid," said Margo.

"Aye, it needs skill and a firm hand."

"Do you live around here?"

"I have a small grottage along the coast. I retired here a few years back. Wrecks are my thing. Marvelous habitat, wrecks. I had an article published recently in the Salvage Review. Perhaps you've read it?"

"No, but that sounds exciting."

"It's Rory, by the way."

Roger coughed. He had been looking out to sea.

"That looks like a nasty squall coming in. Perhaps we should be heading back?"

They all turned to follow his gaze. A dark band was spreading across the horizon. Overhead, the noon sun was now a sickly yellow orb, seeming to hang in the haze. Over the synthetic reef, the air was still calm, but the octopods could sense the building electrical charge. The jockeying of the plastic to which they clung had become more noticeable over the past minutes; it creaked as it flexed. Far offshore, a sharp line separated blue water from the dark, white-flecked sea beneath the low clouds. Matters were rapidly getting serious. No octo appreciates the turbid confusion of a storm, and the disruption that often follows: detached plastic gets tossed about, property markers shift, and wifi service is frequently lost.

The group of protesters seemed to have mostly dispersed: only a lone pair remained. They were still clinging to the edge of the reef when the wind suddenly tore across them, flinging sheets of yellow foam across the reef.

"Those two are looking for trouble. I don't understand those who put themselves at risk, and then expect to be rescued. It's common sense to seek shelter." Margo, some years previously, had thought about becoming a magistrate: she would have known how to deal with such people.

"They seem to be heading back now," replied Devilly, who was watching through binoculars. "There—they've disappeared underwater and will be safe enough in the tunnels. Will you be coming back to the Inn with us, Mr. McKraken?"

"My damn squid has disappeared, so I might as well."

"It might be quicker if we swim underneath the plastic," suggested Anna.

"No, you will get completely disoriented. Best to return by the path you know. I am not even going to try to return to my place to-night—if it is still there after this storm."

It seemed a prudent idea, as a large swell swept beneath them, and millions of cemented bottles arched upwards, groaning under the stress, before sinking back into the following trough with a multitude of sighs.

# Chapter 6

THE RAMBLERS SLID down into the labyrinthine comfort of the plastic, below water and out of the wind. The squall front had overtaken them now, and heavy drops of rain pelted the water surface like shot.

"Just in time," thought Devilly, who had been finding her prolonged exposure to the open air a little trying.

Led again by Margo, who set a confident pulsating pace, they began to retrace the route they had taken that morning. It was familiar going, although the motion required them on occasion to grip firmly with their suckers. When the crests of the waves forced the plastic upwards and above water, the wind whistled eerily though chinks in the plastic. It was a far cry from the pleasant morning swim they had enjoyed outbound.

When they reached the junction with the

main path they encountered the pair they had previously seen from afar. They were hovering, apparently unsure of which direction to go.

"This signage seemed to have spun around," said the elder of the two, a grey octo carrying binoculars and a rucksack. "Do you know the way back to the Inn? We had planned to stay there tonight."

"I have a map," replied Roger. "Good thing I brought it. I don't trust those new GPS gadgets."

"May we join you if you are heading back? My name is van Oesterhuis, Professor van Oesterhuis. And this is Serpitula Argo, one of my grad students."

The young companion grimaced at the mention of her name. She bobbed forward: a young octo in reef camo, almost goth.

"It's Serpie. I carry the Professor's bags."

"Well, I think we should all be getting a move on," said Roger. "Perhaps formal introductions can wait until later."

The enlarged group made it back to the Inn as the storm swept over the outer arms of the Gyre. The wind howled and, looking up, they saw spume driving across the water surface overhead. They hurried inside.

"Everyone in the Lounge!" Mr. Blackpen, the landlord, was hovering in the entrance, still clutching clams with which he had been shuttering the openings to the Inn.

The Ramblers, accompanied by McKraken, Professor van Oesterhuis and his assistant all wafted tiredly into the Bubbles Lounge, relieved to find shelter from the tempest. They had been chased from the promontory by the smack of waves against the plastic cliffs, and the surge of broken water pouring over them. Even though the tunnels provided some shelter from the tumult at the surface, the last stretch to the Inn had been alarming, the trail twisting violently as each wave charged beneath them. Although still early afternoon, it had become quite dark, illuminated by lightning flashes that cast their contorted shadows against the jagged plastic.

"That was a near thing. There was nothing in the weather forecast about a storm blowing in," said Roger, after escorting Margo to a seat. Rory McKraken with Devilly and Anna took the clam bench opposite, snug against the back wall of the lounge where things seemed better anchored. Van Oesterhuis and Serpie Argo retreated to the far side of the faux fireplace in a vain search of warmth.

"It's the time of year," said Mr. Blackpen. "When the Gyre spins into the cyclone track. We've had a few good'uns, I can tell you. I'll just fire up the bioluminescence so we can see."

He reached up and stroked the rows of polyps dangling from the ceiling. They began to emit a sullen glow.

"Now what would we like to drink?"

After some discussion, Roger went to the bar to negotiate with their landlord. The latter was employing several of his arms to tether bottles that were trying to float away in the increasingly violent motion. Roger returned minutes later.

"Here we are. Tea for Devilly and Anna; gin and 'it' for Margo. And a whiskey for you, McKraken."

"That's good of you, Seethe-Mantle," said Rory. "Cheers!"

✧　✧　✧

RORY MCKRAKEN INSISTED on buying the next round, and the one after that. Drinks and conversation helped distract the company from the storm raging outside. Rory embarked on a long story about the Arboreals who used to live in the Scottish archipelago, how they were strangely skirted and fond of bags of wind. Devilly was beginning to find his company tiresome but was amused to see Margo—lubricated by several gins—hang on his every word. He was interrupted by the sudden entrance of their landlady.

"Oh, you poor dears." Cephelia Blackpen bustled into the Lounge, accompanied by her kitchen help. "Now, if there is anything you would like to eat, just let me or Tenta here know. Say 'hello' Tentacula."

The young octo curtsied awkwardly: a little gauche and all arms. She must be barely out of school, thought Devilly.

"Tenta has just joined us from the agency and getting to know our little ways."

"Is it rough in the kitchen, Mrs. Blackpen?"

volunteered Anna. "The wave motion . . ."

"Oh no. We've had storms like this before, havn't we, Blackpen? There is nothing to worry about. But let me get you some soup. Soup will be just the thing. Or, how about some nice lobster smoothies? Or crab cake? Mr. Blackpen always likes a bit of my crab cake, even if I say so myself. Oh, but you must be tired, swimming all that way. I was only saying to Mr. Blackpen that you should have taken sandwiches. You must be starving . . ."

A loud crack, coinciding with a lightening flash, cause the landlady to pause before she had a chance to repeat the menu. The Inn was flooded in brilliant white light that etched an image of the lounge and its occupants on the retinas of the gathered octopods.

"That was a close one," observed Roger, blinking.

"Yes," said Devilly, after regaining control of her ventilation. "If I might ask, Mr. Blackpen, how thick is the plastic under the Inn?"

"Six metres, as they say in the old money. That would be ten tentacles. Good quality bio-cement. Never had any trouble with it. Mind, can't say the same for the new developments. Building with cheap plastic, so I hear. Rich buggers out of Centro. Build where they like, and they have the local council eating out of their hand."

"Oh, and who is the developer?" asked Margo, always with an eye for coastal real estate.

"Bling Construction. Owned by Sir Callas Bling—you will have seen him at the hunt."

"Our so-called Master of Squid," interjected Rory McKraken. "Quite the big fish around here, isn't he, Blackpen?"

"Aye, he is that." Although Mr. Blackpen seemed reticent about talking about Sir Callas Bling, his wife had no such reservations.

"Mr. Blackpen would like to give them a piece of his mind, wouldn't you dear? Only last week we had those so-called friends of his staying. What they did to the sheets, I won't try to describe. Tied in knots, they were. And their manners. Well, if that's how they behave in Centro, I'm just glad we live out here in the country. It's all very well, but when Mr. Blackpen—in the nicest possible way—suggested that they park their vehicules in a more orderly fashion, well I don't know if I should repeat what they said. They called Mr. Blackpen some awful names, didn't they Mr. Blackpen? What was it now? Oh yes, they called him a . . ."

"Aye well, Cephelia," said Blackpen firmly. "I think you have something on the stove."

"Oh my, that's the soup boiling over. It'll taint my water! Oh my . . ."

Devilly gathered that the landlady had strong opinions about this Callas Bling. The surname was familiar to her because of her favourite indie bookshop in Centro where she was booked to do a signing next week. Surely this Callas Bling couldn't be related to Leo? Leo could barely afford the rent, and Devilly sometimes wondered if it was sales of her books that kept him afloat. Running an independent bookshop seemed to her a perilous venture economically.

Devilly remembered reading about Bling Construction. Last year, the company had featured in a news story in Gyre Week, a magazine to which she subscribed. A reporter had written a piece suggesting shady dealings regarding a major government contract. Bling sued, the paper docked a hefty fine, and the offending journalist banished to the travel section of the newspaper.

"Do you happen to know, Mr. Blackpen, how they are pricing the new condos," pursued Margo.

But before he could answer a loud crack resonated throughout the Inn, followed by a chorus of pops and the screech of rending plastic. Suckers clenched around the Lounge.

"Not to worry, folks, we must allow for a bit of give."

The bar was now swaying slightly. Devilly felt they had bobbed closer to the surface. The room seemed to spin. Devilly supposed that it was the disorienting effect of the lighting, the reverberations through the plastic integument from the thunder overhead and the increasingly violent motion. She hoped the spinning was just an illusion.

No illusion, however, was their landlady who re-entered the lounge carrying bottles of soup in her ample arms. She was trailed by Tentacula laden with baskets containing various small crustacea. It took consummate skill to distribute the food, and the company had to snatch it from the water with flailing tentacles.

"Thank you, Tentacula." Rather an old-fashioned name, thought Devilly.

"Oh shit," said Tenta. A violent motion had overturned the basket, sending shrimp scampering for the corners of the lounge. "Hey, I'm sorry. I will fetch another . . ."

✧　✧　✧

"GOOD GOD, WHAT weather! Too damn rough for the hunt. Best get those shutters up, Blackpen!"

An enormous figure had appeared at the door of the *Bubbles* Lounge and Restaurant, an octopod in dramatic silhouette against the lurid glow outside. Undulating its lateral fins, the octo wafted into the lounge, if such an imposing figure could be said to waft. Once inside, all could recognize the Master of Squid, still dressed in a vulgar pink that—Devilly felt—clashed with the pattern of blue rings on his skin. A smaller octo entered the lounge behind him—slight and darting—but hung back in the shadow by the door.

Looking up crossly at the intrusion, Mr. Blackpen straightened abruptly, and substituted his habitual scowl for an ingratiating smile. He swiftly emerged from behind the bar, wiping his welcoming tentacles.

"Ah, good afternoon, Sir Callas. Come in, come in. Sit down, sit down. Here move long Miss." He chivied Anna and Devilly to move further along the bench on which they had been reclining. "Sit ye down, Sir Callas. I have just the thing for you 'ere: a special malt. Swept from the shallows ten revolutions past. The label is still just visible. Peaty, as you like it."

"Good God, Blackpen, you have quite a gathering here," said the new arrival, accepting the drink, and surveying the others in the lounge. "Ah, there you are, McKraken. Thought we had lost you."

"No thanks to you, Master. You might consider lessons on how to lead a hunt," rejoined McKraken, holtly. "Some Master you make. I never saw such a ragged affair."

"As you know, McKraken, taking the squid

out in weather like this was always a risk. But I seem to recall you were one of those who insisted. Didn't come just to fish from the bank, I recall you saying. So if you think ..."

McKraken's colour had warmed to a fiery scarlet. The dark figure who had followed Bling into the Lounge eased forward.

"That's all right Tako-san," said Sir Callas. "I'm sure Mr. McKraken is just upset. It was certainly rough out there today." Then, noting the presence of ladies, the newcomer smiled and turned towards Devilly.

"Callas Bling, at your service. Master of Squid. You may have seen us out in the sound earlier? Yes? Good sport with the mackerel, but sadly no porpoise today."

McKraken snorted and turned to the bar, where he rapidly adopted the peat-stained cast of the nearest whiskey bottle.

Roger, a little bewildered, coughed and introduced the Ramblers.

"Nether Vortex? Can't say I've heard of it. But first things first. Thing is, Blackpen, it seems we have detached from the Gyre. Just returning from the hunt the squall caught up with us. More of a hurricane really, and the waves tore apart the outer fringes. My place is spinning out there in the storm somewhere and you have broken free too, Blackpen. You havn't looked, I suppose? *Bottlings* is no longer attached, and spinning free in mid-ocean, ha ha!"

"I'd best slide out to check," muttered Blackpen.

I was right, thought Devilly: we are spinning faster, and in the opposite direction to the Gyre! She was used to the Gyre turning slowly, driven by lazy tropical currents in a clockwise rotation. Octopods habituate to this steady circulation—a revolution takes about a year—and automatically adjust so they know which way is North. Now all was confusion: the Inn and its immediate surroundings had broken free, an isolated swirl of plastic; a satellite of flotsam orbiting the Gyre. It was all most confusing.

Blackpen returned.

"Aye, we've broken off, right enough. I'll go and see if there is anything loose in the cellar."

He slid behind the bar and disappeared

down the hole leading to the lower levels.

"Not to worry," said Sir Callas. "After all this has calmed down, the emergency services will reconnect us. I have no doubt about that; it's what we pay taxes for."

"Could we swim for it?" asked Devilly. "Back to the Gyre, I mean. It can't be too far."

"I would not advise that. We let the squid loose at the end of the hunt." Bling looked at his watch.

"And it's their dinner time. Voracious creatures."

# Chapter 7

Although small talk trickled on for another half an hour or so, all assembled in the lounge were tired after their days exertions: the attraction of bed became ever more beguiling. Sir Callas Bling was the first to excuse himself. He drained his glass.

"Well, Blackpen, I think you are stuck with us for the night. Do you have a room available?"

"Indeed, Sir Callas. The Jeroboam. It may be a mite cramped for you, mind."

"Oh, don't worry about that. I am sure we can manage. Tako can sleep in a winkle, if he does ever sleep, which I doubt. Good night, all!" And with much the same flourish as his entrance Sir Callas departed the Lounge.

To the landlord's relief, Bling's departure triggered a general exodus; he didn't have to call "Time" and could close the bar earlier than usual.

"Just how big is the Jeroboam, Mr. Blackpen?" asked Devilly as they were leaving, curious to know. It had not been offered to them on arrival, yet it had been given to this Bling character without hesitation. Still, she supposed, it was an emergency.

"Eh? That would be four bottles, Ms. Peen. It's our honeymoon suite."

Now Devilly, from her beachcombing days, was familiar with the kinds of flotsam one might expect to find around the edges of the Gyre. A Jeroboam would be a rare find indeed, and more likely to find an honoured place in a local museum, not for bedding honeymooners in a pub.

"Surely not a real Jeroboam bottle, Mr. Blackpen?"

"Real? 'Course its real. Real plastic. Bought it at a fire sale years ago."

✧    ✧    ✧

BACK SAFELY IN the Annex and tucked into *Beaujolais*, Devilly hoped for a decent rest. In vain: the night was uncomfortable, and it was not until the early morning hours that the jiggling of her sleeping bottle eased, and she managed to catch a few hours sleep. When she descended to the lounge for breakfast all seemed calm, and she gratefully helped herself from the small buffet that Mrs. Blackpen had provided. She was tackling a second small crab when Anna appeared, looking a little worse for wear.

"Morning. What a night!" Anna collapsed on a clam. "My bottle never stopped rocking."

"Yes, it was uncomfortable," replied Devilly. "Still the storm is over now. Mr. Blackpen found rooms for both that Bling fellow and Rory McKraken. I hope they weren't adjacent."

"I expect McKraken found a bed in that whisky bottle—after he had finished the contents of course! And Bling? Where did they put him?"

"In the honeymoon suite: 'Jeroboam' I believe it's called. Don't ask: it's a fake."

"How suitable: I'm sure he will feel at home. What happened to that sinister fellow who was with him?"

"Something in the servants' quarters, I believe."

They both sipped their morning coffees with some trepidation, the quality of the contents of the plastic pods being described as "vigoroso" on the label. It did not taste much different from seawater.

The events of the previous day was still milling about their various minds. Anna completed the round of her eight subsidiary brains first, and commented: "You should consider yourself lucky, Devilly. You must realize that we have here the perfect set-up for a murder mystery: a group of strangers trapped on a spinning country inn surrounded by murderous sharks ... they disappear mysteriously, one after the other ..."

"Oh, very funny. I just finished one book and I am completely tied up trying to market the thing. I am supposed to be at a signing next week. I really needed this break to recharge. And we are supposed to be surrounded by squid, not sharks. At least, according to Sir Callas. One can argue with a squid: they are not unreasonable creatures. Sharks on the other hand, have been around so long they think they own the ocean. Famously stiff vertebrates, they just can't appreciate a mollusc's point of view."

"Yes, and I suppose we are not all strangers. You and I have known each other for ages, and Margo and Roger are friends of yours. Do you know them really well?"

"Yes, we play bridge together."

"I see. You must know all their secrets then."

Of course, thought Devilly. And she had been corralled by Margo to help judge at various villages fetes, but now she thought about it, their conversations had seldom penetrated deeper than discussing the quality of someone's sponge cake. And Roger? He had, since retirement, so thoroughly assumed the role of retired gentleman hobby farmer that it was hard to imagine him as anything else. A dull ornament, frankly.

Speak of the devil, thought Devilly as the Seethe-Mantles appeared at the entrance to the Lounge. "Morning Margo. Morning Roger."

Reunited, the Ramblers huddled around a corner table to rehash the adventures of the previous day. A little later, van Oesterhuis entered, acknowledged Margo's hearty greeting with a distracted nod and went to the buffet. He retreated to a corner table with a pickled sea cucumber. There, he sat alone, munching slowly and reviewing a sheaf of what to Devilly looked like examination papers. Of his student there was not yet any sign.

"Not the chatty type, our good Professor," murmured Roger. "Does anyone know what he is a prof of?"

"I gather he is an expert on the sociology of marine ecosystems," replied Anna, quietly. "I recognized the name. I've read a review recently of a paper he published called *Choreography of grievance in dance moves of the Common Cuttle*, or some similar rubbish. I think he was being interviewed on the radio only the other day."

"That's a bit harsh, Anna," said Devilly. "It's a fascinating field."

"I just don't like people who lead with the "I'm a doctor". When I'm on holiday, I don't go around insisting on Doctor Teuthis this and Doctor Teuthis that."

"Well, maybe you should," interjected Roger. "At least you are a real doctor, Anna. Even if your patients are mostly dead, ha ha!"

"Mostly?"

"I mean, well, I meant . . ."

"Shut up, Roger," said Margo. "Ah, here comes Mrs. Blackpen. I could do with a refill."

The landlady bustled into the room from the kitchen, juggling an assortment of food baskets. On seeing the Ramblers, she paused.

"Oh my dearies. What a morning! And that Tentacula chooses today to disappear, of all days. What can one do. I'm being run off my feet, in a manner of speaking."

"Is there any more coffee, Mrs. Blackpen?" asked Margo.

"Coffee? Breakfast is one pod per guest; Mr. Blackpen is very conscious of waste. How about tea? We have a wonderful house tea, if I do say so myself. Now, I can't stay to chat. Run off my feet, I am. Where has that wretched girl got to?"

After sampling the house tea the previous evening, no one was inclined to repeat the experiment.

"Looks like we are left to our own devices," said Devilly. "How about a quick tour outside to see the damage. I heard Blackpen say our Inn had severed from Crabster village and is adrift."

She uncoiled from her clam shell and drifted to the door. In passing, she asked Professor van Oesterhuis if he would like to join them. He looked up from his papers, a little bemused at being addressed.

"Oh, no, I don't think so. I'm waiting for Serpitula."

"We'll let you know if we see any cuttles dancing on our stroll."

"What? Oh, you know my work?"

"We had heard that you are an expert."

"Indeed? In that case, I may accompany you. There have been some interesting developments in the field, to which in all modesty I myself have contributed. I think I have a draft of my latest paper here somewhere, should you wish to read it." He scrabbled through the documents on the table. "I must have left it upstairs. I will just slide back to my grotto and fetch it."

Professor van Oesterhuis retrieved the papers he had been working on from beneath the remains of his breakfast and jetted from the Lounge.

"Now you've done it," observed Margo. "We'll be bored to death after ten minutes."

"It seemed the polite thing to do," said Devilly, hovering uncertainly in the hall.

# Chapter 8

A CHOPPY SEA spat across the surface of the raft, making exposure to air tolerable as the Ramblers plus Professor van Oesterhuis ventured outside to explore their predicament. The dowsing with spray was quite agreeable, but frequently obscured the view.

Viewed from sea level, the curve of the earth ensures a near horizon; the white peaks that Devilly could see across the water could not be far distant. They were—she soon realized—those very peaks that they had been watching so intently the previous day. She could even—without binoculars—make out the swirl of birds around them. The sun was just breaking over the horizon—a brilliant band of red below dark clouds. The guano islands glinted in its rays; briefly, before the sun rose higher, they looked like blood-kissed meringues.

Devilly knew that *vorticelle* was the technical name for a circular raft of plastic detached from the continent of garbage that constituted the Gyre itself. Last night's storm had ripped away the vorticelle to which they now clung. A mere two hundred metres in diameter, it spun slowly about an axis of thickened plastic that betrayed the presence of their Inn just below the surface. Devilly gave silent thanks for the industry of encrusting barnacles that had allowed the old structure to weather the storm. Well-cemented and thickened over the years, the Inn had withstood the violent flexing; otherwise, they might have spilled into the ocean in the middle of the night. Their accommodation now formed the hub of a spinning wheel of plastic.

Behind the Inn and still intact was a shallow depression filled with loose un-cemented plastic garbage. It seemed that Mr. Blackpen had given permission to camp, and a filamentous tent suggested that certain refugees from the storm had taken shelter there.

"That will be some of the environmental crowd we saw yesterday," said Roger. "Blackpen mentioned that a couple of them had stayed on after the protest. It must have been an uncomfortable night. Now, I think we will go this way . . ."

Roger and Margo were determined to circumnavigate the vorticelle in an anticlockwise direction. Anna, stubbornly, wanted to explore clockwise, and to prevent any acrimony, Devilly suggested that they agree to meet up on what would be the leeward side in an hour or so.

The group of three set off against the wind, slipping and sliding across the plastic towards the sea. The motion of the raft was quite lively—much more so than on the Gyre proper—and required the frequent application of a stabilizing sucker. Devilly guessed the raft was only a few tentacles thick at most, and here and there, gaps in the fabric seemed to penetrate to the dark ocean depths below. However, the bright cool morning was bracing, the views were stunning, and Devilly forgot her disappointment over the meagre breakfast.

Devilly suddenly froze. There before her, swimming lazily in a shallow pool confined in a sheet of plastic was a sea slug, placidly munching on a growth of sea lettuce. She recognized the species of nudibranch from its flamboyant colouration; it undulated its deep purple flanks like a Roman senator and waved multiple pink gills, frivolously advertising its toxicity.

"Careful," she called as van Oesterhuis swam up behind her. Following Devilly's pointing tentacle, he stared down into the pool.

"Ah, yes." Oesterhuis coughed and bent down to examine the specimen closely. "Normally pelagic, of course, and I presume swept here by the storm. Quite fascinating."

"Do you know what kind this is?" asked Devilly, ready to allow the Professor to confirm her identification. She had already recognized the genus—one of the family of black slugs—but identification to species level needed an expert.

"I would say it is a *versicolor*. Completely harmless, of course. Now, I don't suppose either of you thought to bring a sample bottle. My assistant usually carries sufficient, but Serpitula seems to have overslept this morning."

Devilly, a keen student of marine life, was deeply shocked. She did, as a matter of fact, carry a sample bottle in her poison sack, but she was not about to satisfy the Professor's collecting urge. She drifted away to join Anna at the very edge of their plastic raft.

"That man seems to think a black slug is harmless," she whispered. "*Versicolor* my foot—I know something of sea slug poisons myself, and that one is deadly. Granted it was dressed in innocent summer colours, but the nonchalant way it moved with no care for predators is characteristic. He might be a professor of something, but he is strangely ignorant for a marine biologist."

"Well, I told you *cuttles* are his field."

"That is no excuse."

They slid arm in arm along the margin of plastic, bracing each other against the surge.

"I'm surprised we haven't seen Bling and McKraken," remarked Devilly. "I would have thought they would be the types to get up early, if only to renew combat."

"Fair weather huntsmen, I imagine," replied Anna. "Sir Callas is just a city type who enjoys playing the country squire. He is much more comfortable in the board room."

"Oh, do you know of him?"

"I know him too well. We met at University. 'Cally' Bling he was then, the male lead in our amateur theatre group production of Romeo and Juliet. Quite a dish. Destined to join the ranks of the shakers and movers."

"Do you think he recognized you?"

"Yes, I expect so, or at least he is wondering why I seem familiar. We had a thing going for a short while back then."

"You are a dark horse, Anna. So why not a joyful reunion of old friends?"

Anna gazed out to sea, scanning the horizon.

"Youthful indiscretion. Even back then you couldn't be sure if he had a moral compass. And since then, there have been scandals and rumours, not to mention several messy divorces. Recent revelations in the papers of Bling's holdings in offshore tax havens have tarnished his reputation."

Better not to push further, thought Devilly. If Anna wants to tell her more, it would be in her own good time. She looked down into the water, her suckers firmly attached to the edge of their island raft that jockeyed in the still muttering sea.

The jagged plastic edge bore testimony to the violence of the storm that had ripped them from the Gyre. Always a keen collector of glass floats and tupperware, Devilly had long been fascinated by these mute witnesses to the civilization that preceded the octopods on the planet. Scholars had written treatises on the subject, and Devilly was conscious that her knowledge of the runes frequently found imprinted on these objects was woefully limited. But here, among the usual mish-mash of pop bottles, carrier bags and foil wrappings, a pattern of six caught her eye: a six-pack of cans, tethered by plastic collars. They kept buoyant, so she guessed, by air trapped inside. She reached down and examined one of the cans. The labeling was still legible, and she could make out several letters—"Something something *CLASSIC*." Who knew what that might mean? When she tightened her suckers on the can it exuded a thin stream of dark rust-coloured liquid. Out of curiosity, she tasted it with a tentacle: a bitter brew indeed, and she wondered if the Arboreals consumed much of it.

A sudden shout made them both look up. In the distance, on the opposite side of raft, they could see someone waving.

"That looks like Roger and Margo," said Devilly.

"Is that Roger beckoning to us?"

"We had better go over and see what they want."

Leaving van Oesterhuis to his collecting, they skittered over the plastic to rejoin their fellow Ramblers. In contrast to what was currently to windward, this trailing edge of the vorticelle sloped gently into the ocean. Until they span further around, this side would be sheltered from the waves. When they came up to Margo and Roger, they found the Seethe-Mantles staring down into shallow water. Following their gaze, Devilly saw only a tangled mass of plastic and weed, but Anna was quick to point out the mangled remains of an octopod bobbing in the water.

Quite suddenly, the confusing patterns in

front of Devilly resolved into eight twisted arms and a pulpy body, intertwined with a long strand of sargasso kelp. It was already drawing the attention of the cleaners; battalions of sea lice were swarming towards it.

"Here, Roger. Pull on that arm while Devilly and I lift it clear. I won't allow evidence destroyed by the nibblers on my watch. A fine weekend break this is turning out to be."

It had been some time since Devilly had watched her friend at work, and that had been in the antiseptic surroundings of the central morgue. She had forgotten how Anna's banter while she cut up the cadavers had grated on her at the time. Not to mention her insufferable bossiness. After all, Devilly, as a writer of crime fiction, was familiar with dead bodies and could tell as well as anybody how long the . . .

"The camouflage is still sharp. I would say between six and eight hours. Do pull harder, Dev. It's not going to come apart!"

With a concerted heave Roger and Devilly, under Anna's direction, hauled the corpse back onto thicker plastic. By now, they were puffing from their exertions. Being in the open air was uncomfortable, but fortunately the weather was overcast and the air moist and cool.

"Let's be having a closer look," said Anna. "Devilly, just hold that arm up, will you. A little higher. Good." Anna stooped over the body, caressing it with a tentacle, and retrieving a scalpel from the depths of her mantle.

"Never travel without my kit," she commented, seeing the surprise on the face of her audience. "Devilly, if you have a notebook handy, you might want to take down my observations."

Fine, thought Devilly, pulling out a plastic scribbler. Of course, I always have a notebook handy. Why wouldn't I? But further speculation had to wait, as Anna launched into a rapid staccato.

"Female, young I would say under twenty well nourished, colour—well put down motley, evidence external trauma—bruises around the siphon, suckers on tentacle retain some scraps of skin—sample bottle please Devilly. Now, let's see inside, shall we?"

"Oh really! Must you do that here, Anna?" cried Margo, who had been watching with increasing discomfort. "Roger, don't let her cut it up here!"

Anna paused, her tentacle raised for the first incision.

"No, I suppose I don't have to do this *al fresco*. But we should carry her back to the Inn quickly. Decomposition is so rapid in this climate that the quicker I do the autopsy the better. But a few minutes won't make much difference, and I can work under calmer conditions at the Inn."

As if to second Anna's thought, a wave slapped the edge of the raft and drenched them all. Thank you, ocean, thought Devilly.

"We need something to carry it in," said Anna. Roger, who had been poking around in the plastic garbage, pulled out an old bin bag.

"This do?" he asked.

Together, they tipped the remains of the unfortunate girl into it. As they did so, an arm of the corpse dropped free.

"Wait!" cried Devilly. "Wait—that looks like a tattoo. She leaned close. It's a text!—a bit smudged but I think it reads 'One of something Thousand.' What do you think that means?"

But Anna had gone pale.

"That is the crowd I was telling you about, the ones who are calling me the spawn murderer. 'One of a Thousand' is what they call themselves."

"I am sure it is just a coincidence. It is a group of activists—those types attract young people. Getting a tattoo is usually as far as it goes. Even if the tattoo is significant, you could hardly be the target. How could they possibly know that you are staying here at the Inn? Mrs. Blackpen said that her kitchen help Tentacula had been with them for two weeks."

"I don't like coincidences. You didn't get those letters. They were quite vile."

Devilly hadn't seen the letters, but she had read an article on "One of a Thousand". They had been involved in several demonstrations in Centro, and she remembered that they were active in several different causes, usually protests against the Establishment. As a movement, they seemed to be an eclectic mix of pro-lifers offended by government restrictions on egg production, environmentalists, and back-to-organic plastic originalists. The media painted them as having outlandish views, such as trying to revive some of the ancient practices of the Arboreals—drugs, for instance.

"Remember the hunt protesters?" said Devilly thinking back to their hike of a couple of days previous. "I bet there might have been several in a thousand among them. I myself am sympathetic when it comes to porpoises."

"Yes, if it's about the hunt, I could understand them protesting Callas Bling. I would join in on that."

"There you go then. Nothing to worry about as far as you are concerned."

Still, Devilly could see that her friend was upset. Perhaps she felt guilty about flushing most of her eggs all those years ago. It had not occurred to Devilly that her pragmatic, professional friend was suffering from remorse to the extent that she might think she was being persecuted.

# Chapter 9

ON THEIR RETURN to *Bottlings*, they found Tako-san in the foyer, wilting under the tongue of their landlady. Unable to defend himself against her verbal assault, he was bowing profusely.

"Room service?" screeched Cephelia Blackpen. "Room service! Where do you think you are, some fancy 5-star hotel in Centro? You are asking me, with my condition, to traipse back and forth carrying this, that 'n' t'other to your precious Sir Callas as if I have nothing better to do all day. You can take a tray from the kitchen, if you must, but UNDER NO CIRCUMSTANCES are cuttles permitted to mingle with the other guests, so keep to the back... oh, hello dearies. Back from a swim around the island, are we? Such as nice morning for it after all that weather last night. I never seen the like, I was saying to Mr. Blackpen.

What do we have there then?"

Roger had floated the bulging bin bag containing the remains across the sill and let it settle to the floor in front of the landlady. The others hovered uncertainly in the entrance.

"Bit of a turn up, actually, Mrs. Blackpen. We found a body."

"Well, about time. I'll give that girl a piece of my mind. Causing all this trouble for the guests and leaving me to do the necessary this morning. Where is she then?"

Anna intervened, her tone briskly professional.

"No, you don't understand. We have found a *dead* body. Now, I need two things: a table to work on for the autopsy, and access to a freezer afterwards. Mrs. Blackpen?"

But the landlady had turned purple and was ventilating rapidly.

"Oh, my saints," she gasped.

"Are you well, Mrs. Blackpen? This must be a shock for you, perhaps a glass of water?"

Devilly slipped into the lounge and took a bottle of Perrier water from the fridge behind the bar. She returned to the foyer to find their host recovering quickly. Mrs. Blackpen waved away the proffered bottle. Eyeing the sagging bag, curiosity overcame her initial disgust.

"Is that our Tenta, then, in that sack? Poor little thing. Oh, Mr. Blackpen will be distraught. What a shame."

"We don't know who it is yet," said Anna. "I am a doctor and can assure you that as soon as I can make a proper examination, I hope to identify the deceased. Would you feel able to identify Tentacula, or perhaps Mr. Blackpen?"

"Oh dear. Well, she was not with us long. A pale little thing, as plain as plain if you ask me, but flirty with the young men, if you know what I mean. Only arrived this past week lookin' for a summer job. What with all the extra liftin' and carryin' with Mr. Blackpen's bad back, and now all the laundry 'cos the washing machine is broken, and Mr. Blackpen insists he can fix it, but he hasn't yet, so we took her on with no references."

"Do you recall any particular marks that might confirm her identity?"

"She was covered in tattoos when she arrived, but fade those out, my girl, I said. Our guests don't want to be served by someone inked up like that."

"A tattoo could be helpful. But, as I said, there is nothing yet to confirm identification. It could be some unfortunate carried off by the storm from the mainland."

"Well, she's gorn, our Tenta, ain't she?" Mrs. Blackpen sniffed and looked hard at the bag. "Take that into the laundry room then, but it's not going in my freezer, whatever you may say, Miss."

# Chapter 10

"**I**'LL THINK WE'LL sit this one out," said Margo after she and Roger had helped Devilly and Anna lug the body into the laundry room. They left it floating mid-water.

"Rather," said Roger and both headed back into the lobby.

"They will be wanting a drink, I imagine," said Anna, watching them depart, and fumbling in her mantle for her glasses case. "Not that I blame them. Autopsy is not everyone's cup of tea. Still, I'm glad you are staying, Devilly. You will be a great help. Now, catch onto that bag." Seeing her friend put on her reading glasses reminded Devilly that Anna was a little ashamed of being very long sighted. Octopods have extraordinarily good vision but in Anna's case corrective lenses were necessary. Merely the addition of black-rimmed spectacles made Anna look severe, professional and scientific.

Devilly snagged the floating bag and helped Anna wrestle it to the floor.

"You seem to have got over seeing that tattoo. It was very faint—I may have misread it."

"Yes. And it will have faded away completely by now," replied Anna, in her professional tone of voice. "Nothing to worry about. Now, let's be having you." She reached into the bag and pulled. The body hung in the water, before Anna pushed it firmly to the floor. "Hold it down, will you?"

With the body held down by Devilly, Anna began her close examination.

"Seven—no, eight—slashes on the arms. Deep, possibly fatal." Anna probed the wounds with a thin ruler. "Hard to say what made these: could be teeth, or claws. The ragged edges tend to rule out a knife. Or not."

"Perhaps a bread knife?" suggested Devilly. She might as well have been talking to herself.

"The lack of discolouration suggests that these are post-mortem. So, we must look for a different cause of death. You would be surprised, Devilly, how hard it is to kill an octopod," continued Anna, ruminatively. "Our bodies usually absorb any blow with a blunt object, and one can usually recover from anything other than a decapitation; limbs can be regrown. I had one the other day with a shark bite that had torn away half of the head. Suffocation is quite common and . . ."

"What about poison?" asked Devilly.

"Yes, poison. But let's not get ahead of ourselves. Let me just slit this mantle."

Anna applied her scalpel, and the water took on a greenish tinge.

"Tweezers?"

Devilly passed the instrument.

"Aha!" Anna slowly extracted a strip of pink plastic bubble wrap from the deceased's siphon.

"There, the fatal ingredient. It was most likely suffocation."

"Could it be self-inflicted. A suicide?"

"Unlikely. There are plenty of plastic bags floating in the water here, and Mrs. Blackpen has ensured that there is no shortage of bubble wrap around the Inn. It could be accidental inhalation. But how did she get those gashes? They don't look like shark attack to me—the tell-tale crescent shape is absent. No, I think she must have been slashed with a sharp hook."

"What about Humboldt Squid? I read that their have tentacles tipped with claws, and Sir Callas mentioned that they have been known to attack octopods at certain times of year."

"Really? Let us say, for now, death by misadventure, possibly caused by an encounter with wildlife."

"I'm still supposed to be taking notes, am I?"

"Oh, Devilly."

"Don't worry. I have been recording all your wisdom on my dictaphone. I can transcribe them later."

Anna and Devilly exchanged looks.

"All right," said Anna. "You want to test for poisons. Go right ahead. I know you are dying to try out your kit."

Devilly, in pursuit of veracity in her crime writing, had made a study of marine venom. She had even published on the subject, although *Playfish: Wreck and Reef* hardly counted as an academic journal. Over the years, and after extensive experimentation—some detrimental to her health—she had trained the tip of one tentacle to detect various poisons and venoms. This proved a useful—and possibly life-saving—ability for Devilly.

Her discriminating appendage had helped the police on several occasions. Local officers in Vortice Main understood that Devilly Peen was the aunt of a high-flying Chief Inspector in Centro, and they had learned to tolerate her uncanny ability to turn up at crime scenes. To the frequent frustration of investigators, the morgue was often backlogged, and seldom able to produce even a preliminary report with any speed. Devilly could identify a poison at the scene, giving police a head start on finding the perpetrator.

In most cases, Devilly's opinion would be confirmed by later analysis. This, in truth, peeved the official pathologists who liked to work methodically in the laboratory, where they had a sterile environment and a patient passively awaiting their attention. Anna, although regarding Devilly as a good friend, was not immune to being irritated by interfering amateurs.

Devilly inserted the tip of her sensing tentacle into the crop of the corpse. She could taste something, but it would take her brains some time rummaging through their archives to identify the substance.

"Well?" asked Anna.

"Faint, but it is definitely there," replied Devilly. "A low concentration, but that it to be expected after she has been washing around for hours."

"Yes?"

Devilly pulled back her tentacle and turned to her friend.

"It's a tetrodotoxin: a very faint whiff, but definitely there."

"Oh, come on. Are you saying that she ate a pufferfish? I don't recall pufferfish on the menu of the high-end sushi restaurants in Centro, let alone at some chippie here in Crabster."

"No, but the bite of the blue-ringed octopus contains a similar venom."

"I think I'll wait for the laboratory analysis before we start accusing anyone, thank you very much!"

It seemed to Devilly that the laundry room, that had seemed quite warm, had suddenly become chilly. She bit back a sarcastic retort and prepared to explain calmly to her friend that, even when diluted by alcohol, the drug had a distinctive flavour. She had barely opened her mouth to speak when the clam that they had used to close the door was thrust aside, and the bulk of their landlord surged through the opening.

"What's this then? Found a body, have we? Mrs. Blackpen says its our Tentacula."

Blackpen hovered over the table where Devilly and Anna were examining the corpse. He was a large octo and cast the victim into deep shadow.

"Please get out of the light, Mr. Blackpen," said Anna.

"Pitiful," said Blackpen, continuing to hover. "Aye, that's our Tenta. Pitiful."

"When did you last see her, Mr. Blackpen?" asked Devilly.

"Oh, let us see now. That would be after the storm last night. Poor thing was quite shook up and we gave her a wee drink to buck her up."

"It could be useful to know what she had to drink," said Anna.

Blackpen looked a little embarrassed.

"Come on, man. What was in this drink?"

"Why, truth be told, after we close the bar, we squeeze the dregs from all the bottles into a big plastic bag, then add coffee and sugar. It sets one up like nothing else."

"So, you've been adding to this bag over days, weeks?"

"Eh? Wot's this about then? She was fine, perky even, and she said she was going for a swim. That's the last I saw of her."

"No matter," said Anna. "But I expect the police when they arrive will want to interview us all."

"Police? What police? Why it was just an accident of nature, they are saying. Attacked by a Humboldt no doubt. The open water around here is swarming with the vicious creatures. No need to report an accident of nature, surely? We can't have the police crawling all over, disturbing the guests."

"It won't be up to you, I'm afraid, Mr. Blackpen," said Anna. "I am a forensic pathologist, and this is a case where the police must be informed. It may, as you say, be an accident of nature, as you say, but murder is also a possibility."

"Murder! Oh, pull another arm, it has bells on. You'll be saying the murderer is one of our guests next. And here we are, surrounded by ocean teeming with Humboldt Squid that would tear you apart as soon as look at you. Or sharks, plenty of them about as well."

"There are marks on the body, Mr. Black-pen. It might be the wildlife, but—as I say—it is too early to tell."

"Swimming for her life, she must have been, and the heart gave out. Anyways, you won't be getting your precious police here any time soon. All the lines are cut: you can forget express bottle—they don't pick up on week-ends."

"In that case, we will have to find a cool place to store the deceased, somewhere secure where the shrimp can't get to it. You wife was adamant that we couldn't use the freezer."

"Oi should bloody well think not! We have all our crab in there. Where are we supposed to put those, I ask you? Anyways, the freezer stays shut until the power comes back on."

"I see," said Anna. "I hadn't remembered about the power being off. In the meantime, perhaps, if you could find an empty Tupperware for the body, that will have to do."

# Chapter 11

IT WAS ALMOST a funerary procession that entered the Lounge of *Bubblings* half an hour later. Mr. Blackpen led, bearing before him a large plastic container. He was followed by Anna and Devilly, cast briefly as mourners.

As they came in, Devilly glanced around. Margo was there, in conversation with Rory McKraken, while Roger was at the bar chatting with Mrs. Blackpen. By themselves in the corner, van Oesterhuis was sitting with Serpie Argo. He glanced up at their entry, and hastily withdrew a suckered arm that was draped around his research assistant.

Talk died to a whisper as their host deposited his burden on top of the bar. Visible through the transparent sides of the box, a row of suckers pressed against the side advertised its macabre contents. Everyone had known that Anna had been in the laundry room examining the body retrieved from the surf, but they had not expected it to be presented in such fashion. Some had already ordered dinner, and this did not sit well with the several orders of crab-in-a-basket that Mrs. Blackpen had placed on the serving hatch a moment before.

"Oh, my Gord," groaned the latter on seeing the box, all the while fiddling with the till. "Here's your change, Colonel. Thank you kindly, I'm sure . . ."

She turned to face her husband. "You can't leave that 'ere, Blackpen. It ain't decent!"

Anna slid forward to placate the landlady. "Dear Mrs. Blackpen, since the power is off, we really need to use the ice box under the bar to keep this fresh . . ."

"Well, I never heard of such a thing!"

With that, she withdrew to the far end of the bar, going a deep puce, arms waving and with the skirts of her mantle billowing in exasperation.

✧　✧　✧

WHILE BLACKPEN RELOCATED the contents of

the beer fridge under the supervision of Anna, Devilly draped a towel over the Tupperware box containing the remains. Having done so she turned, to find the occupants of the lounge staring at her expectantly.

Devilly was a well-known author of detective fiction. Her lively amateur detective, Daisy Cuttle, had featured in numerous best sellers in the mystery genre. Devilly knew they assumed that she, as the creator of Daisy, would also have the nous to solve a murder, however intricately planned. They expected an early demonstration of Sherlock Holmesian intuition. Intuition be damned, she thought. What she would die for right now is a cup of tea.

With their entrance, all the guests of the Inn with one exception were gathered in the *Bubbles*, sprawled across the plush furnishings, arms twisted into postures that aimed at nonchalance but betrayed their anxiety. This was understandable: after a stormy and uncomfortable night, they had awakened to discover themselves marooned on a spinning disk of plastic, somewhere offshore the mainland Gyre. To top it all, they now shared the Lounge with a corpse.

"Still no sign of Sir Callas?" she asked, as she slid into the space between McKraken and Margo on the plushly upholstered clam.

"Ashamed to show his face, I imagine," said McKraken. "That meet yesterday was a disgrace. You know, it is only his money that made him M of S. The man has no feel for squid. They need a firm whip hand."

"Oh, have you been hunting porpoise a long time, Rory?" asked Margo.

"Long enough: I've a wee place along the sound. Bought it when prices were dirt cheap. Aye, I've been riding with the Humboldt for years. Used to be a local event. Now with all the city people coming out here, and buying up the property, you get all sorts trying it out. Useless in the main part. Worst thing is that the local folk—the fishermen who have been here since Splashdown—can't afford to live here anymore."

"We saw all those new condos going up as we drove into the village. Is Sir Callas Bling really building a resort development out here?" asked Margo. "How are people supposed to find it? Our drive was horrendous."

"Knowing C.B., he'll have some government type in his pocket. I heard there is talk of a new tube line all the way from Centro; City to Crabster in less than forty minutes. It'll be the end of the place, in my opinion."

# Chapter 12

To Devilly's eye, the late morning sun filtering through the water at the entrance to the lounge cast a pleasing effect of rippling greens and yellows against the walls with their motif of rose-tinted sea squirts. Squirts were a choice that Devilly would not have tolerated back home in Nether Vortex, but here melded well with the ambience of the Lounge.

The guests had got over the shock of seeing the body served at much the same time as lunch. Mrs. Blackpen's crab portions had been unusually generous, and the subdued burbling of postprandial chatter lent a degree of normality to their situation. Mr. Blackpen was working the coffee machine behind the bar at a steady rhythm, and most of his guests were mollified, sucking at comforting after-lunch cappuccinos.

Devilly sat with Margo and Roger. Margo was holding forth on how decent seaside cottages had been priced out of reach. It was an all too familiar refrain, and Devilly was barely paying attention.

"Beg pardon. Sorry to intrude."

The deferential whisper came from beside Devilly's ear. She looked around, and for a moment saw nobody, only what at first glance appeared to be one of Mrs. Blackpen's patterned rugs.

The rug gathered itself, spread its arms, and drifted to hover in front of her. Suddenly, it blinked and resolved into a rotund octopod in a rumpled suit.

"Do I have the honour of addressing Ms. Peen?"

Devilly had been impressed by the camouflage, but now she had a clearer view, she realized that octo had hardly needed to make the effort: it was as shabby as the carpet it had risen from. The eyes that gazed at her expectantly—blood-shot and wreathed in wrinkles—matched the colour of the faded anemones worked into the pattern.

"Yes, I am Devilly Peen. How may I help you?"

"Septic Hagfish at your service, Ms. Peen, of Hagfish and Offal, Solicitors." With a speed that belied the slow unraveling of a moment before, the octo presented a business card to Devilly by a tentacle tip.

She examined the plastic.

"You are based in Centro, Mr. er Hagfish?"

"Indeed, indeed. Our offices are in the Bling Tower. I am by way of being the senior partner."

Devilly was amused, imagining this decrepit creature sharing space with the sharp young octos she saw filing in and out of offices whenever she was in Centro. Amused and curious.

"You seem to know my name, Mr. Hagfish."

"Indeed. I should explain. My client, and the reason for distracting you from your party, is a great fan of your work. I would venture to say, perhaps your greatest fan."

Which was gratifying, but one didn't send one's lawyer to ask for an autograph. By now, Devilly was both curious and uneasy.

"May I ask who . . ."

"If perhaps we could retire to somewhere a little more private?"

Devilly glanced at her friends. They had stopped their conversation and were listening intently. Margo was scenting scandal.

"Of course, Mr. Hagfish, we can go to the drawing room. It is this way."

✧   ✧   ✧

OUT OF EARSHOT, Devilly turned on Hagfish, and demanded to know who he was representing.

Hagfish coughed apologetically.

"My client apologizes for having taken this opportunity to approach you in this manner. He believes that here at the Inn, you may be able to provide a service for him."

"A service? But you still havn't told me his name!"

"A well-remunerated service."

"Mr. Hagfish, I am getting annoyed with your evasions."

"His name is C.B. Bling."

"Bling! You mean the Bling Tower Bling? The financier?"

"Indeed."

# Chapter 13

D ESPITE HAGFISH MUMBLING, Devilly was sure that everyone had gathered that she was to be granted a private audience with Sir Callas Bling. Devilly imagined hostile stinging tentacles aimed at her back as she followed the lawyer from the room. She couldn't blame theme: this was all most irregular, and why should she be singled out?

In the hallway of the Inn, Devilly hesitated, unsure which way to turn.

"Sir Callas is waiting in the Jeroboam Suite," said Hagfish, turning left past Reception and pulsing down the narrow corridor that led to the Inn's interior accommodations. Here, it was clear that Mrs. Blackpen's taste prevailed: more plastic ducks illuminated their progress and the cheap plastic walls had been painted pink with spangles. They swam past several closed clams, including the door to the grotto called Magnum where she might have stayed except for the mix-up about rooms.

At the end of the corridor a bouquet of sea-weed swayed in the slight current above a picture of *Bottlings* rendered entirely in tiny sea snails. Hagfish turned left, and they glided along another passage that sloped downwards into the thick midden of waste that formed the deep foundation to the Inn.

Down they went, and down. She let one arm trail along the wall feeling a change in texture as they passed from light plastic—much still filled with gases—to glass jars and bottles. The foundations had been carefully laid to ensure sufficient buoyancy and went much deeper than Devilly would have guessed from the mild topography at the ocean's surface. But, before she could give much thought to the physics of this construction, Hagfish stopped before a large clam set into the wall. Above the entrance "The Jeroboam Suite" was engraved in a romantic font.

"Sir Callas has been looking forward to meeting you," whispered Hagfish, with an expression that Devilly could only describe as a smirk. He knocked, and Devilly faintly heard an acknowledgment from within. The clam swung open, and Devilly came face to face with Bling's valet. He was as black as ink.

Ushered inside, Devilly found herself floating in a large grotto. It was furnished with over-stuffed puff plastic sofa and armchair in the faux-Arboreal style Devilly had seen in magazines. Recesses along one wall contained a large screen, a mini-fridge and a nook for an elaborate coffee maker. Devilly certainly did not have one of those in *her* room.

A chair of ergonomic design had been placed before the large porthole that ran along one wall of the grotto. The view was of blue water some ten metres below the surface of the sea, and Devilly glimpsed a platoon of small fish at work kissing the glass to keep the window clean of algae. The chair's occupant had his back to her and appeared to be working, hunched over a low table with a glass top. On Devilly's right, an archway led into the bedroom where she glimpsed an extravagantly large sleeping bottle beside an untidy swirl of sheets. Clearly Bling had not thought to tell his valet to tidy up for her visit.

After several moments had passed in silence, Sir Callas Bling rose from his chair, his purple rings aglow, and turned to her.

"My dear Ms. Peen, so good of you to accept my invitation." He waved an arm in greeting. "Pay no attention to him," he continued, noting Devilly's nervous glance towards the black octo, now hovering behind her. "Tako-san is my constant companion and I travel nowhere without him. He is also my sushi chef and a master of knives: he can carve any kind of seafood with precision—very useful for odd jobs."

"'Tako'—that's a name from Fuji Archipelago, is it not? Doesn't it mean 'Octopus'?"

But, receiving no response from Tako-san, Devilly was left pondering what the odd jobs might entail. Bling laughed and gave a grand belch of welcoming affability.

"Tako is invariably mute. Now, I won't take your arm because—as I expect you know—I am harmful to touch. It is the curse of the blue-rings."

Devilly was sure she had the antidote

tucked away somewhere in her mantle. Almost sure. She pulsed slightly backwards to preserve the distance between them.

"Please sit and make yourself comfortable," said Bling, his arms gesturing towards the sofa.

Devilly arranged herself on the soft couch, and she settled deeply into its folds. Bling returned to his ergonomic chair and swiveled towards her. This gave him the advantage of dominating height.

"I am a great fan of your books, Ms. Peen. I have read all your Daisy Cuttles and am a great admirer of your wonderfully complex plots."

"Well," said Devilly, surprised, "if you wanted a signed copy, I am sure that could have been arranged with less drama, simply by contacting my secretary, Anemone."

Devilly words implied a rebuke to Bling's legal advisor, but the lawyer had discreetly withdrawn, a mere wisp of ink hanging in the water the only sign that he had ever been there.

"Sir Callas, I think you need to explain your behaviour, and not only to me but to the others who are presently gathered in the lounge bar. I am sure they are discussing you at this very moment, and not in a complimentary way."

"Ha. Yes. Firstly, I want you to understand, Ms. Peen, that you are the reason that I have—as you say—caused you all to fulfill my wishes and congregate here at the Inn."

"That is very flattering, I suppose, but entirely mysterious. Also, if I might say so, extremely presumptuous. I am here with my friends on a bird-watching expedition. The sighting of a Bling—however rare a bird he may be—is not on my agenda."

"On the contrary, Ms. Peen, I don't believe you for a moment. Your latest book *Serial Suckers* names me. I am the unfortunate who is murdered first—whose corpse provides the playground for your amateur detective to showcase her deductive skills."

"My new book hasn't been distributed yet—I am supposed to have a book launch this week—so you couldn't possibly know . . ."

"*Sir Callas Bling meets his untimely end*—it says so on the back cover. At least you had the courtesy to give me the title."

"But it wasn't you: my character was called

something completely different."

Suddenly, Devilly felt unsure of herself. She recalled the strange conversation she had with Anna when they were driving to the Inn, about a character from earlier in the series ending up on the mortuary table.

"Look for yourself." Bling reached behind his desk and suckered the top copy from a crisp stack of brightly coloured plastibooks. He proffered it to Devilly. She saw immediately that the lurid cover screamed murder mystery: it was definitely one of hers.

"I had my people arrange for these to be removed from the bookshop of my good-for-nothing nephew Leo. It was there, I believe, that you hoped to have your launch?"

Confused, Devilly slit open the plastic covers and began to flip through. It *was* her novel, and there on page two was the name *Callas B. Bling*.

"It is a pretty good plot," continued Bling, "and I do, as you describe, own many buildings in Centro. But, real estate aside, my interests lie in several other directions. I am a major supporter of the Arts, for instance. But, this really won't do: I have a reputation to uphold, and certain of my less literary competitors might take advantage of my fictional death. That, I cannot have. Besides, I have no intention of dying."

"I really have no idea how this could have happened."

"You have a rare talent, my dear Ms. Peen. Your creative process is formidable. I am truly astonished."

"That is very flattering Mr. Bling, but I can only say that I had no intention of putting you in this position. In fact . . ."

Yes, in fact, what could possibly have happened? She had dictated the manuscript using her new machine, reading from her written manuscript, and then given it to her secretary to transpose. True she had not checked the text later, leaving that to Anenome. To be honest, she tired of reading her own work, and relied on others to bring it up to scratch. When they had received the proof copy, she had given it barely a glance: Anenome had assured her that Wordscribbler gone through it with a fine-toothed comb and caught 95% of the typos. Well, there were always some that slipped through. But why? She forced herself to concentrate on what Bling was saying.

"Ms. Peen, as you must know, I am very wealthy, but wealth brings its inconveniences—the need for enhanced security being one. I have made many enemies: most I have ensured remain impotent, but all need to be reminded from time to time that my bite is worse than my bark, should they be so foolish as to attack. The image of power keeps the sharks at bay."

"I can see that, I suppose," said Devilly.

"Of course you can! You are famous as well in your own way. You must have annoying fans always chasing after you."

"Well, no. Nether Vortex is a bit off the beaten track, and readers tend to assume I am called Daisy Cuttle, after my heroine."

"You are being modest, I am sure, Ms. Peen, or may I call you 'Devilly'?"

"I would rather you didn't . . ."

"Now, Devilly, let me explain something about myself. I am, as you must realize, a *Cephalo*. After my grandfather arrived on

Splashdown Day, he fell in love with an indigenous octopus, one of the pure-blood blue-rings—quite the local aristocracy. This was in the early days of our settlement when we were still corralling plastic in the open ocean and welding it together into rudimentary habitat. Strange isn't it, how species from different planets can breed and produce healthy offspring, yet for those evolving on the same planet such unions are infertile? I'm sure the science boffins understand."

Bling paused, gathering his thoughts.

"I am half blue-ring, and as a young octo, I am ashamed to say that I used the threat of my bite to build my empire. But that was in the early days; now I have employees to do the rough stuff."

People like Tako-san, thought Devilly. "I still don't understand what you need me to do."

"Simple: you must alter your manuscript."

"You mean swap your name for someone else? I suppose I could do that." Devilly had suddenly remembered the name she had originally thought of, one *Slipper Batch*.

"What? No, that wouldn't do at all. I am

honoured to be in one of your novels. It is quite … titillating. No, what I would like is a complete rewrite to change the plot and the ending."

"But here? At the Inn. How am I supposed to do that?"

"Blackpen will arrange everything."

"Our landlord? Why should he do that? I don't think he likes you very much."

Bling gave a barking laugh.

"No, you are correct: he hates my guts. But, you see, I own him; the Inn is mine, his livelihood is mine. So, I'm not really surprised: it is useful to know one's enemies—it is one's friends that are the problem. They can—as we blue-rings say—change their spots in a flash."

It was, Devilly supposed, gratifying to find that someone like Sir Callas valued her work, but surely, he had more important matters to worry about? Why was he so concerned? It was fiction, after all. The important thing was that he didn't seem about to sue her for defamation.

"I really dislike having to alter a story, Sir Callas. I am cross that you saw fit to stop my book launch, but I admit that you had reason.

Although I really have no idea how you came to be named in my novel, I suppose I could try to develop a new plot."

"Good. Just remember that Tako keeps me safe. He is a master of martial arts. You may have heard of the octopod double punch? He practically invented it. He is from the Japan Islands—the Fuji Archipelago, as you cleverly deduced."

Devilly had been practicing the double punch for years but had only graduated to orange belt. The Japan Islands lay in the western Pacific. Although she had never been, she had seen the travel brochures: tiny volcanic peaks poking through some of the most tremendous banks of plastic in the ocean. The Japanese Arboreals, it seemed, had been particularly productive in the distant past.

"Sir Callas, if I do as you ask, I must warn you, the creative process is unpredictable: I might fail. And, in the last analysis, it would be up to my publishers. They might reject the new manuscript."

"I don't believe that for a moment, Devilly. You are your publisher's gold seam: he is bound to publish. And should he initially decline, well, I can't imagine him refusing after receiving an invitation to my island. Now, where has Hagfish got to? Ah—there you are!"

The lawyer materialized beside Devilly. A master of camouflage, Hagfish had managed to blend perfectly into the furnishings.

"Septic here has something for you to sign. It is always best, I find, to have a written agreement."

"You mean you want me to sign a contract?"

"Just for clarity, my dear. Septic, run through the main points for Ms. Peen. You really don't mind if I call you Devilly?"

❖   ❖   ❖

I WILL HAVE to sign, she thought, having read through the document with care. The contract had the usual clauses although twenty-five percent of royalties seemed unreasonably steep. She beat Bling down to the usual ten. He was just pretending to be a literary agent, he had said, laughing. Only the final clause on non-fulfillment puzzled her.

"What damages do you envisage if I find myself unable to deliver?"

"We don't need to consider that eventuality, do we? It is a mere hypothetical," said Bling, dismissively. "I have no doubt you will succeed. By the way, before you leave *Bottlings*, I want Tako-san to show you his knives. I insist you watch him carve a fish—his speed and skill must be seen to be believed."

There it was—the naked threat, and Devilly was relieved when Bling rose and escorted her to the door.

"Hagfish is braving the passage back to the Gyre today. I try to discourage him, but he insists that he has an understanding with the Humboldts—they are still fasting, so I hear, and the seas remain perilous until after they feed again. Still, Hagfish is too distasteful to be bothered by the squid and will doubtless outwit them. Should any contractual matters arise, you may contact him at Bling Tower. Now, please enjoy the remainder of your stay here, Devilly. Should you feel that more birdwatching would help you write, ask Blackpen to arrange transport: my properties border the sanctuary, and I allow no common tourists to disturb the nests. I don't suppose hunting porpoise is your thing? No? Well, let's keep that for another day."

# Chapter 14

THE INN SEEMED strangely quiet when Devilly found her way back to Reception after meeting with Bling. That was all to the good, she thought; she needed to retreat to her room and think, but the thought vanished as Mrs. Blackpen rose from behind the counter.

"Oh, Ms. Peen, I am so glad to have caught you. If you don't object, we are serving dinner in the Public this evening." Mrs. Blackpen was quite apologetic. "It is much closer to the kitchen, you see, and we are short of staff for reasons that you will understand."

"I am sure that will be quite all right," replied Devilly. "Do you happen to know where I can find my friends?"

"Mr. Blackpen has closed the bar in *Bubbles*, so they all went to the Public. As I was saying to Mr. Blackpen, it ain't right that the guests have to go to the Public, but he says there is no public at the moment anyways. And then there is that, that thing in the Tupperware." The landlady looked nervously towards the arch leading to the Bubbles Lounge.

✧ ✧ ✧

I WOULD WELCOME a change of scene, thought Devilly, tired of seeing plastic ducks marching across that faux fireplace.

Pushing through a curtain of weed, she swam down the short tunnel—toilets to the left, kitchen to the right—beneath an arch and into the Public. This proved to be a largish cavern, roughly hacked from dark plastic. The water itself changed flavour, from the pleasant tang of ozone in the Lounge to that of rank seaweed. Here the taste of Mr. Blackpen took over from that of his wife: photographs of fishing parties with grinning and overweight octos holding up their prized catch decorated the walls. A snap of a younger Blackpen, in sporting colours, testified to his prowess at ink-blotting. Rows of beer cans—trophies from garbage-raking competitions long past were stuck to the glass behind the bar.

Overhead, screens filtered the sunlight so that the bar stayed dim, and she found herself facing a gigantic screen on the far wall. Squid racing was on. That she would soon find the muttering voice of the commentator irritatingly persistent, Devilly was in little doubt. She felt that she had wandered into a different world— a more masculine world of sports teams, spilled beer and sticky seats.

A few high tables with uncomfortable look-ing perches were scattered across the room. They seemed to be constructed—rather crudely—from corks and screw-on bottle tops stuck together with bio-cement. Devilly wondered if making furniture provided the creative outlet for Mr. Blackpen. The effect was a robust counterpoint to the rather twee decoration in the Lounge.

Around the cavern walls ran ledges for addi-tional seating. Someone had dragged a couple of the tables together beside the ledge, and it was here that she found her fellow guests.

"About time you showed up," called Anna, waving, as Devilly entered the bar. "Over here, there is space beside me if Roger would squeeze up closer to Margo, and Rory—why don't you find another chair?"

Anna was describing for the table an old murder that had occurred in a suburb of Centro. She had performed the post-mortem on the victim: it had been particularly gory, and Anna was describing to her captive audience in vivid detail the wounds on the victim. She was obviously being "good value" and rising in Margo's estimation. Devilly had heard the story before and felt that her friend applied a little too much dramatic licence to the mundane job of cutting and slicing. To Devilly's certain knowledge most of the blood would have drained from a corpse before Anna got her hands on it. Now—according to her—she was up to her arms in gore and blood. They would be ordering Bloody Caesars next, to go with the seaweed snacks.

Van Oesterhuis at the neighbouring table gave Devilly a cursory nod and returned to lecturing whom she assumed to be a pair of hunt protesters, refugees from their encampment in the garbage pool. They huddled on the ledge, arms interlaced. That made them hard to count; she thought only two, but their mutual choice of green camouflage didn't help to distinguish the individuals.

Rory McKraken was offering to buy a round.

"A tea would go down well, thank you Rory," said Devilly.

"Four Bloody Caesars, please landlord. And a tea."

✧　✧　✧

DEVILLY PERCHED ON a stool at the edge of the group, sipping the house brew, but disinclined to participate in the conversation. She had, tucked into her mantle, a copy of *Serial Suckers*. Bling had given it her, although he seemed convinced that she should be able to remember every line she had ever written; he himself claimed to be able to quote chapter and verse, but then he had reread all her novels several times over. This was the forty-fifth of her Daisy Cuttle series—how anyone could possibly think that she could recall all the plots, characters, ingenious devices and deductive intuitions: it was ridiculous. When she tapped "The End" on the manuscript, she was already planning the forty-sixth. Her editors and proofreaders would take over the tiresome business of getting it print-ready. For Devilly writing books was a business: she had no wish whatsoever to reread her own work for pleasure. When not writing, the garden and her curiosity about other people filled her time. She had once overheard someone behind her at the checkout call her a nosy busybody. What nonsense! It was just research.

Now, if she was to obey Bling's wishes, she would have to refocus her mind and juggle the plot, all the while making Sir Callas something of a hero, and a surviving hero at that. Bling's ego made that difficult. Any normal person would, she felt, be delighted with sharing a name with the victim in one of her novels, but it seemed he wanted to be a heroic survivor and the detective as well. It was a bit much, and it occurred to Devilly that she would, in fact, delight in seeing his character perish. If wishes were horses …

What a bore, though; rewrites were the bane of an author's existence.

✧   ✧   ✧

"YOU WERE GONE a long time," said Margo, turning to Devilly. "What did Sir Callas Bling have to say for himself?"

"He said I should consider this perforce stay here at the Inn as a writer's retreat . . ."

"Nice of him. The rest of us can die of boredom, I suppose. No word of when we will be reconnected to the Gyre?"

Not until Bling approves my rewrite, thought Devilly, but she could hardly tell that to the others. Here they were in *Bubblings*, confined to a small island of garbage solely so she could focus on her work. Sir Callas had contrived to bring together a useful cast of potential murderers. Some, she now suspected, resented Bling or held grudges. If not in fact, then motives would be easy enough for Devilly to imagine: van Oesterhuis, for instance, might depend on Bling for his research grant while undertaking an environmental survey to smooth planning approval of a Bling development (weak); perhaps Bling was foreclosing on a mortgage on the Seethe-Mantles' manor house? (Poor Roger.) Or Rory McKraken?—his disdain for the Master of Squid merely a cover for his own ambition (tenuous.) And Anna, of course, seemed to be remembering a "me-too" moment—she of the hidden scalpel. (More promising.) The Blackpens, now: they appeared to be resentful sycophants, but they were country folk with their own dark stirrings. Even Leo Bling—so she now realized—might expect to inherit should Bling die. It was an embarrassment of riches.

Yet Sir Callas expected Devilly to ensure that his character in the new *Serial Suckers* would foil all attempts on his life, and triumphantly bring the murderer to justice. In case Devilly needed a real victim, Bling hinted that he had provided a body—the unfortunate who was resting in Blackpen's beer fridge. If Tentacula's corpse was meant to show Devilly how ruthless Bling could be, it had worked.

On leaving the Jeroboam Suite, Sir Callas was effusive. Should he be satisfied with the product, he would ensure that Devilly's new book launch would have all the fanfare it deserved. Queues would line up outside Leo's bookshop, he assured her. They would be fighting for signed copies. If not, he would buy the entire first edition.

"My dear Devilly," he said in parting, "work your magic and then you can go back to your charming Rose Grottage. Your anenome garden is particularly fine, although I hear that the blue peonies sometimes suffer from sudden die-off syndrome. That would be most distressing for you."

How could he possibly know about her prize blue peonies? She shuddered.

So in reply to Margo, Devilly lied: "He is in the same boat as the rest of us. The local authorities are overwhelmed repairing storm damage. 'How the emergency services prioritize is one of life's mysteries' were his exact words. We might be stuck here for several days yet."

"I suppose it is some compensation that the wealthy must suffer with the rest of us." Margo sounded bitter. "I am surprised he can't whip up some transport to whisk him away to that penthouse in Centro or one of his country mansions."

"Callas said the waters around us are too dangerous. The Humboldt Squid are in their annual reproductive fever. Even the locals know that it is best not to swim in open water at such times."

"Blasted Humboldts," interjected Roger. "Somebody should do something about them!"

"So, it is 'Callas' now, is it?" said Anna. "He always was a charmer, but I'm surprised you fell for it."

"I actually found him quite civil. The years must have mellowed him. Certainly, some of the ruder edges have been smoothed over."

"Once a blue-ring, always a blue-ring," muttered Anna. "A vicious, manipulating bastard under that pretty purple skin."

Manipulative, yes. Determined to have his way, yes. Not averse to the rough stuff, as he called it. Yes. Bling, quite frankly, had frightened her. On the other hand, his desire to be the hero in one of her stories was quite flattering. Despite her apprehension, when she thought of the agency that Bling had given her—a writer's power over her characters—she felt quite smug.

Further discussion was interrupted by Cephilia Blackpen, who bustled in from the kitchen to ask who would be taking dinner.

"What's on the menu this evening?" asked Margo.

"It's the thawed crab, you see. Mr. Blackpen is insisting that we make space for poor Tenta in the kitchen freezer—more suitable, so he says. In my opinion, it's to free up his beer fridge. Crab all round is it, then?"

One way to end all of Bling's potential assassins at one blow, thought Devilly.

# Chapter 15

AFTER DINNER, DEVILLY excused herself. The long summer evening would give her opportunity to write, provided she could find some solitude. Returning to her grotto in the Annex, she swam past the Blue Lagoon and noticed an arbour carved in the plastic. It was set back from her path and had been seeded with hundreds of tiny corals that had grown in an uncontrolled fashion. Now, they almost covered the original structure. Beneath the overhanging polyps was a sheltered nook with a rustic seat and a stump of coral. Here was a secluded spot, she decided, and the stump a perfect platform to work on.

Back in *Beaujolais*, she retrieved her typewriter, a notepad for scribbling ideas, and the packet of inspirational sachets she had brought with her from Nether Vortex. She hurried back to the arbour, feeling the creative tide rising within her. There was not a moment to lose!

Devilly settled herself—machine on the stump in front of her, pad to one side—and took a couple of deep breaths. And then ... nothing. She stared at the plastic sheet in the typewriter—a frighteningly blank expanse entirely free of text. Moments before she had felt inspired, but now all that evaporated like morning mist.

She needed a drink. Although she made a point of sticking to tea in company, when alone and faced with a blank page, alcohol was her friend. Extracting a sachet of hard lemonade from her pouch, she tore off the tab and sucked down half. Almost immediately, she felt the benefit: a sudden ease, and a mild curiosity about the percentage of alcohol in the drink. A school of small fish swam past in smart formation and, ignoring the sign, disappeared down the mouth of the Blue Lagoon. Pretty. A barracuda hurried after them ...

To work, then. She sucked the remaining contents of the sachet and put a second within easy reach.

Bling had set her a difficult task. First, she

had to decide on who the new murder victim would be, if not Sir Callas. Her first thought was to reintroduce the name she had originally thought of, but which had been mysteriously changed in the manuscript. *Slipper Batch* had been a thief and a huckster, promoting shady real estate on the outer isles. The properties he hawked were either sinking or consisted of nothing but acres of blue water. He made enemies.

Devilly thumbed through the copy of *Serial Suckers*. Here it was! On page 35 she described a body grotesquely displayed, eight arms cuffed to a playground carousel like a starfish. In the following chapter, the police identified the victim not as Batch but as Callas Bling, the wealthy industrialist. Also, she noted, someone who made enemies.

Other than being dead, at their recent meeting Sir Callas had strongly objected to the term *industrialist*: "I have many interests, my dear Devilly, but industry is not one of them. I prefer to be called a wealthy aristocrat and patron of the Arts. In your rewrite, I must come across as a gifted amateur detective."

Devilly had protested that she already had a detective—Daisy Cuttle! Her main character ran through the whole series and couldn't possibly be changed. But Sir Callas was stubborn: after forty-five appearances, he insisted, it was high time to dispose of Daisy.

Blast Bling! Still, he appeared to have touching faith in her powers of invention. She had no choice: the threat of being sued was real, let alone the unspecified measures mentioned in the contract. Devilly settled down again, to face the typewriter.

Now, if she was to do this job properly, why not start from the very beginning? Even with Tentacula's corpse safely "bagged", she still needed four more victims for *Serial Suckers*. For all she knew, they might be real people as well, lining up behind Bling for damages if she published. It was safer, she decided, to change all the names.

What were the options? She had done potential murderers, now what about victims? Roger or Margo? The Professor or his assistant? Rory McKraken? Mr. or Mrs. Blackpen? It was always best, thought Devilly, to base an imaginary character on someone she knew firsthand; familiarity allowed her to colour her prose. She briefly considered Anna as victim but rejected the idea: her friend would be much better suited to the role of murderer. She blushed at the unworthy thought.

It was true that on this trip—Nether Vortex solidarity notwithstanding—that Margo Seethe-Mantle's voice had started to grate on Devilly's nerves: it had a certain braying quality to it. Perhaps Roger could murder Margo—the unassuming husband driven to extremes? He would poison her gin and tonic with . . . a menu of possible poisons flashed through her mind before she admonished herself. Margo kill Roger? Much more likely. Driven by passion for Rory McKraken, she would dispose of her unfortunate partner with . . . with one of the antique weapons that hung in the hall of the manor house. And she would feed the corpse to his herd of holothurians. Although they are vegetarian, she reminded herself.

Devilly took another sip of hard lemonade. She needed a plan. Taking the pad, she wrote down the names of all the guests at *Bottlings* in a long column, adding the proprietors and staff at the bottom. She copied the list into a second column. Then she started drawing lines between murderer and victim, victim and murderer. Half an hour later she had drawn a cat's cradle of all the possible combinations.

In her considerable experience writing murder mystery, one trick she had discovered was to put herself in the place of her literary invention—the tough no-nonsense Daisy Cuttle, heroine of Devilly's forty-five books. What would Daisy do? was a question she asked herself that usually allowed her plot lines to untangle and permit Devilly to type unerringly towards The End. Daisy, having stumbled on the juiciest victim, would track down the least likely assassin. In *Serial Suckers* she had wrapped things up in only 200 pages.

But her muse had deserted Devilly. It was starting to get dark; the decorative bulbs illuminating the path to the Annex cast but a feeble glow. With insufficient light to work, she tore the sheet from the pad, crumpled it, and let it float away.

Quitting the arbor, Devilly pulsed gently

back to *Beaujolais*. She was frustrated: all this brainstorming had only succeeded in her concluding that the most desirable victim was indeed Sir Callas Bling—one of the most detestable octopods she had ever met—and just about everybody had a plausible motive for dispatching him. And now, under the implied threat of a lawsuit, she was committed to writing what was essentially a hagiography for this manipulative self-styled patron of the Arts.

# Chapter 16

THE MOOD OF the guests at *Bottlings* improved somewhat with the news that the company had reconnected the telephone service. At Anna's insistence, the first call out must be to summon the emergency services and the police.

"I'm not taking the responsibility, Mr. Blackpen; it is your duty to inform the authorities!"

The landlord demurred, loss of trade being foremost in his mind.

"Surely, this was an accident, Dr. Teuthis? Do we really need the police? Our high season is only just beginning and this sort of thing . . ."

"I havn't come to any conclusion, accident or otherwise. A murder might attract visitors—people relish the frisson, don't they Devilly?"

Devilly—whose quiet residence in Nether Vortex had become a pilgrimage for her fans whose morbid fancies seemed insatiable—agreed.

"You will be swamped with reservations, Mr. Blackpen. Mind you, should Anna decide that it was only an accident, health and safety will be all over you."

Blackpen made the call, only to be informed that officers would arrive from the nearest police post as soon as possible, but he must realize that with current sea conditions it might take some time.

Devilly heard the landlord exclaim "I bloody well know that" and slam down the phone.

"They are sending someone as soon as they can," he muttered on returning to the group. "In the meantime, they said not to touch the body."

"Did you tell them that you had Dr. Teuthis here with you?"

"Well, of course I bloody didn't. Did you think they would say, sure—go ahead and bag the body and poke around as much as you like? Not: I don't think 911 care if you were the Queen of Sheba."

"Oh," said Anna.

To change the subject, Devilly suggested getting some air. Her glance outside had confirmed that the day was overcast, with a light rain pattering on the skylight in the lounge. Outside would be quite pleasant, in or out of the water.

"Honestly, I think I will take a pass, Devilly," said Anna. "I have paperwork to get through before the police arrive."

# Chapter 17

CONSTABLE TOM GRUNION enjoyed his Saturday mornings at the police post on the Outer Gyre. He had the Saturday squid racing to look forward to, on which he might venture a small wager following close scrutiny of form. Also, he was not at home, where Mrs. Grunion would have insisted that he tackle several chores that he had escaped doing during the week. His dear Lucilia had prepared a long list.

So far it had been a tranquil morning. The excitement of a storm was usually followed by a period of reflection for the small rural community. The usual drunk and disorderlies from the previous evening's revelries were sleeping it off in the cells. Both would be sent home in due course. A possible house breaking had turned out to be nothing more than the excessive creaking of weak plastic that had alarmed the occupant. Even the speed trap had caught nothing more than a couple of wild squid, too young to drive, who had been returned to their parents with the usual admonitions. Theirs was a small community and policing relied on a bit of give and take with the locals.

Tourists on the other hand were fair game: everyone hated the weekenders and city folk from Centro. Grunion was expected by the locals to be their instrument of retribution. Nabbing a weekender for an obscured plate on their camper, busting rich youth for noisy partying in their parents' cottage, or reading the riot act for lighting a barbecue—it was fire season for the love of God, and here they were surrounded by plastic; these were the staples of the Sergeant's routine. When the telephone rang from Centro, the astonished Grunion took several seconds before he recognized the voice of his boss, Inspector Hardcrabbie, and metaphorically sat up straight.

"Yes sir!"

"You know *Bubblings*? It's on your patch."

"Sir?"

"Get over there. We have a report of a suspicious death at the Inn. Lock 'em down, guests and staff, until my team arrives."

"Immediately sir."

"And Grunion. I don't want any slip-ups."

"Yes, I mean no, Sir. Definitely not."

✧ ✧ ✧

THAT'S A PERFECTLY good day ruined, thought Grunion as he backed the police pulsejet out of its tempo. He had remembered to grab his sandwiches and thermos of coffee from his desk before leaving, and these sat on the seat beside him as he dived down the tunnel that led to the ocean beneath. Once free of plastic, he set course for the White Islands, twenty minutes at cruising speed.

Reports this morning mentioned that a large vorticelle carrying the Inn had detached from the main body of plastic during the storm, and that the repair crews had still not succeeded in reattaching it. That was a common enough occurrence out here on the outer arms— people were relaxed about decoupling—but it meant a choppy ride through open water. He had no concerns about wildlife, a pulsejet being tough enough to brush past any he might encounter.

Once clear of the keel of the Gyre, Grunion touched the controls and rose to the ocean surface. He expected to see Crabster dead ahead. He crested a swell and looked around for the errant Inn. There it was! *Bubblings* floated a little east of where it should be, and he adjusted his course. Grunion knew the Inn well; Ted Blackpen was a chum from school, and the Grunions had been there on their honeymoon. That was when it still catered mainly for locals and was called the *Chip and Crab*: now with the influx of city types, prices had gone up and the quality of food down.

Cutting back the pulse rate of the cruiser, he started to drift around the vorticelle looking for a place to land. It was going to be tricky: most of the edges were ragged plastic, and in the chop looked uninviting. Finally, on the leeward side he found a spot where the plastic sloped off into the water. He eased the pulsejet inshore and grounded it on a jostling beach of polystyrene insulation. Unknowingly, he had just parked his police vehicle on top of the scene of crime where Tenta's body had been recovered.

Grunion flicked on the siren to announce his arrival, then slipped off the cruiser, and started slithering across the plastic sward towards the Inn. He was almost there when a large octopod emerged from the entrance.

"'Morning Tom. Glad it's you," said Black-pen, gripping tentacles.

"Ted. It has been a while. What is this fuss about, then? I hear you've got a body."

"Yeah, one of our kitchen staff. Silly cuttle went swimming when the squid were in heat. Now, it's a shame we had to bring you all the way out here for a stupid accident. Covered in squid slashes all over, she is. But we have some lady doctor from Centro staying with us, and she is making a nuisance of herself. Says the death is suspicious. I hope you can clear it up quickly."

"From Centro, eh? Don't know our country ways, do they?"

✧ ✧ ✧

"YOU SAY YOU had it on ice, Ted?"

Constable Grunion was in the Bubbles Lounge with Blackpen. The landlord had just retrieved the Tupperware box with the remains of Tenta and placed it gingerly on the bar countertop.

"Well, Tom, you know the missus. Couldn't have it in the freezer, so it has been in the beer fridge."

"Mm," Grunion peeled open the corner of the box, causing a greenish mucous to shoot into the water. He rapidly fanned backwards as the taste of decay permeated the Lounge.

"Phew! You need to set the dial on your fridge down a few degrees, Ted. This is putrid."

Blackpen, relieved that none of his guests were present, hurried to open the shutters so the current could swirl through the room.

# Chapter 18

**"I** HAVE YOUR statements, so that all I need for now." Grunion was addressing the assembled guests in the lounge "You may all go to your rooms or stay here. But please remain inside the Inn: the seas outside are dangerous."

Anna had collared the constable when he first announced himself. The officer had examined her credentials and been unimpressed. That's as maybe, Ms. Teuthis, he had said, but I have my duty. Sit down with the others, if you please.

"When do you expect the team to arrive from Centro?"

"All in good time," said Grunion, who was beginning to enjoy himself. "Now, Mr. Blackpen has given me a list of all the guests. We seem to be missing, let me see, a Tako and a Bling."

He turned aside to Blackpen.

"Ted, where is Sir Callas?"

✧   ✧   ✧

DEVILLY WAS FASCINATED. She had observed police methods on several occasions from the viewpoint of a professional crime writer. It was important to get the details right in her Daisy Cuttle procedurals, and she was always open to improving her knowledge. But here was an officer who promised to top the list for incompetence. That he was local and seemed to have at least a nodding acquaintance with their landlord she understood, but he had made a farce of his statement-taking. In the end it was a free-for-all with everyone contributing to each others' statements. It now seemed that most of the guests had assisted in pulling Tenta onshore, and Grunion appeared to suspect that Anna might have delivered the fatal blow with her scalpel.

Devilly watched their landlord—who was behind the bar polishing a glass—mutter something to the policeman. She assumed that Bling was in his Jeroboam Suite, and that

Blackpen would know that too.

"Cephie, dear," called Blackpen loudly back into the kitchen. "Come out here an' lend a hand."

Mrs Blackpen appeared, flushed and bustling, as usual. She seemed to be in the middle of shelling a crab. It hung limply in her arms, claws agape.

"Constable here needs to see Sir Callas. Would you show him to the Jeroboam Suite."

"Can't you see I'm busy, Blackpen? Who do you think is going to feed all these good folk, now I'm on me own in the kitchen, if it's not one thing tis t'other, and you forgot to break the claws again. Oh, hello Tom, how's Lucie and the littl'uns?"

"Not too bad, Cephelia. Not bad at all. Mind you, the cold this winter had her rheumatism playing up, but then we're all getting older."

There must be a lot of this in community policing, thought Devilly. Perhaps she should move things along.

"I know the way to Sir Callas' suite, officer. I can show you."

"Ah," said Grunion. "Right then."

"I'm coming too," Anna squeezed out from behind the table.

"We wouldn't want to miss this. I'd love to see the Jeroboam," added Margo. "Wouldn't you Rory?"

"I guess I'll come along too," grumbled Roger.

After some confusion, Devilly led Grunion out of the Public Bar. Trailing them, in a pulsating line, were the Nether Vortex Ramblers plus McKraken, Oesterhuis, and the pair of green hunt protesters. Nobody, it seemed, wanted to be the sole customer left in the Public when there might be a murderer about. Seeing the bar empty, Blackpen looked at his wife.

"Small sherry, dear?"

"Don't mind if I do, Blackpen."

✧　✧　✧

AT THE CLAM barring the way to the Jeroboam Suite, Devilly paused.

"Here we are, Constable."

Grunion pushed forward through the crowd

and rapped hard with a tentacle. The clam swung slowly open in the slight current.

Devilly, peering past Grunion's shoulder, had expected Tako-san to open the door in his silent fashion but there was no sign of the valet-cum-bodyguard.

Grunion advanced into the suite.

"Sir Callas?" he called. "It's the police. I want a word with you about a body. Are you there?"

There was no response, and as Devilly, followed by Anna and the rest filtered into the suite behind Grunion, the silence seemed to deepen. There was barely a sound, even the clicking shrimp—normally tiresome at this hour of the day—had fallen silent.

The Jeroboam comprised an entrance foyer, a master bedroom with *en suite* facilities, a smaller room for staff, and a large salon where Bling had interviewed Devilly. The water was stuffy: clearly Bling did not favour fresh currents in his private apartments.

The office being empty, Grunion slid over to the bedroom door. He seemed to brace himself, and, with suckers attached firmly to the door frame, propelled himself forward.

"Sir Callas, just a quick word if I may . . . Oh Lord!"

Devilly—close behind the constable—glimpsed the Jeroboam bottle itself. It was reputed to be a luxurious bed, with heated water and large enough for quite a party. But now, curled up inside in a complicated knot, suckers pressed against the transparent plastic, was a pulpy mess of octopod. Devilly thought she recognized Bling—despite the contorted arms and squashed features, the blue rings were all too apparent.

"Oi then, I'm sorry sir Callas. I had no idea, if you would excuse me . . . Stand back! you lot and give them some privacy."

"He is dead, you idiot," said Anna, who had pushed through the crowd to examine the Jeroboam. Look, the screw cap is on the bottle: looks like suffocation—only a few minutes of oxygen once the cap is on tight."

Devilly meanwhile was counting the arms visible through the plastic walls.

"I make it at least nine, Anna. There must be more than one body in there. Looks like.you are going to be busy, Constable."

Grunion groaned—it seemed certain now that he would miss all of the Saturday sports coverage.

Devilly's feelings were mixed. More death at *Bottlings* was distressing, naturally, and one felt for the victims. But, on the other hand, Bling had been an odious alpha blue-ring, delighting in making others squirm: he wouldn't be missed. He had boasted about his personal security, and now it seemed that he had ignored basic precautions and jumped in bed with someone. The ego of the man! On a positive note, Devilly had barely begun the rewrite Bling had demanded. Now she could relax: she had written his death into *Serial Suckers*, and now reality had added the full stop. *Fin!*

✧ ✧ ✧

"I SUGGEST YOU secure the scene, Constable," said Anna quietly. "Do you have tape?"

"Tape?" said Grunion, confused by the request. "Tape—yes, we need tape."

He fumbled inside the mantle of his uniform and pulled out a large roll.

"Stand back. Move along now. Nothing to see here. Pardon me." Grunion, exhausting the lines learned by rote from the police manual, collapsed shuddering onto the floor of the grotto, the blue of his authority fading to the pale grey of the faux-coral floor. "Oh, my Lor'," he muttered.

"What an embarrassment!" said Anna. "Devilly, you take one end and I'll tie the other to the cupboard handle."

It did not take them long to delineate an area around the Jeroboam with scene of crime tape. Draped over the furniture like bunting, Devilly thought it gave a festive air that was wildly inappropriate. And now, here was Anna the professional taking charge again. She insisted that no one approach the bottle.

"Don't open that, Roger!"

Out of the corner of her eye, Devilly saw Roger Seethe-Mantle moving to open the porthole. But Anna was too late, he turned the handle, and fresh ocean water wafted into the suite, dispelling the cloudy fug.

"That's better," he said. "Now we can all breathe."

And flush the suite of clues, thought Devilly.

# Chapter 19

"FOR THE RECORD," said Dr Teuthis, "I am taking responsibility."

"Don't you think you should wait, Anna?" suggested Devilly. "At least until the detectives arrive from Centro?"

"No, dissolution waits for no man, let alone the police. I have a duty to do the post-mortem as soon as possible. You know perfectly well, Devilly, that at this temperature octopods decompose in hours, leaving little possibility of identification, let alone a trace of any of those poisons you are so keen on."

"On your head be it. In my experience, the murder squad gets upset when one cuts up a victim before they arrive."

Anna glanced around the suite. Hanging behind the tape, several of the guests of *Bottlings* had failed to follow Constable Grunion's earlier instruction to evacuate, and crowded at the entrance to the suite, watching Anna peering at the screw cap on the bottle.

"I rather suspect their wrath will fall on the constable," she said. "Now, let's get on with it. You were so helpful with Tenta." She gave Devilly a sweet smile.

Well, thought Devilly, multiple corpses in a weekend seemed excessive for a country inn, and one didn't have to appear so enthusiastic about them. Friendship is fine, but when someone reaches for her scalpel with such glee, perhaps a measure of prudence is order.

❖  ❖  ❖

THE JEROBOAM ON its elaborate cradle lay horizontally, although a mechanism allowed for the head of the bottle to be raised and lowered. The neck was relatively slim, but the bottle itself contained a prodigious amount of fluid. In this spacious bedchamber reposed the corpses of Callas Bling and his unknown companion. Already, by this stage of decomposition, Bling's rings had faded to a sickly mauve. Postmortem gases were inflating both bodies, and, with their increased buoyancy, they now bumped against the topsides of the bottle.

Although eager to get on with it, Anna was, at first, stumped as to how to proceed. As city pathologist, she was used to corpses arriving at the mortuary in various stages of decay, but they they had always been extracted at the scene by the emergency services with tools such as the Jaws of Life, although, given the outcome, the name was invariably inappropriate when they arrived on Anna's plate.

"You will have to remove the cap first," called Roger, stating the obvious.

Anna gripped the cap with her suckers and twisted. No go.

"Let me," said Roger eagerly, ducking under the tape. "It is all a matter of leverage."

Devilly rummaged in the pockets at the back of her mantle, sure that she had one of those useful instruments for removing lids from cans. This, she produced with a flourish as Roger, red-faced, was forced to concede his place.

"Good for you, Devilly," congratulated Anna, as she took the tool and broke the cap free.

Anna unscrewed. "Hold this for me, will you? Don't lose it, it's evidence."

Devilly snatched the bottle cap and stowed it deep in her mantle. Of course, she was not going to lose it.

"Now," continued Anna, oblivious to her friend's sensibilities, "now that we have access, I am sure the Inn must have a suction pump." It seemed likely. Most establishments needed to pump up from time to time to adjust the flotation should too much plastic get water-logged.

"I'll go find Blackpen," said Roger, feeling that, as ex-military, he had been trained for this kind of emergency. Besides, it would make a change to give the orders; Margo, for once, seemed struck dumb.

"I won't be long, my dear," he said, briefly touching Margo's arms. He understood things must be overwhelming, even for his wife: it was, after all, supposed to have been a bird-watching weekend, but golly, weren't things looking up!

It was, in fact, some while before Roger returned with the landlord lugging a heavy-duty suction pump between them.

"I dunno," Blackpen was saying, as they maneuvered the equipment with its attendant hoses and extension cords into the Jeroboam. "You say the doctor needs a vacuum pump for Sir Callas? Is he stuck or something? That'll be a first: no one has ever got stuck in the Jeroboam: smaller bottles sometimes, but soap will usually do it. Now what all this?"

Blackpen stopped on the threshold of the bedroom, taking in the scene.

"Yes, he's dead, Mr. Blackpen," said Anna. "Now, did you fetch the pump as I asked?"

"Yes, here it is," Roger chipped in. "They use it for cleaning the guest rooms at turnover. It has a double vortex for extra sucking power and will suck it out in no time. I ordered one myself for cleaning out the holothurians and . . ."

"Yes. Thank you, Roger."

Devilly supposed that Roger had already explained the reason for the request and that was the reason that Blackpen was taking the news so calmly. A guest dead in the Inn's finest accommodation, and in a compromising liaison, as it seemed, with some cuttle! Yet here was their landlord, phlegmatic in the extreme, as he pulled the pump under the scene of crime tape and examined the neck of the Jeroboam to see how to attach the hose.

"I have all the attachments," muttered Blackpen, barely glanced at the contents. He screwed a hose connector onto the end of the Jeroboam. "Aye, this one fits."

"Was this real champagne, Mr. Blackpen?" asked Devilly. She had assumed that a Jeroboam would be corked.

The landlord looked a little uncomfortable.

"It's more ecological than cork," he grumbled. "Elsewise you have to drink the whole bottle at once. Anyways, a Jeroboam is a Jeroboam, even if it is a cheap fizz. No one complains after the first bottle."

✧  ✧  ✧

DEVILLY HAD NO wish to see Bling and his companion unplugged and disentangled; the suction pump had been fitted to the mouth of the bottle, and Blackpen was applying himself to the handle. She heard Anna tell him to go steady, and that she only need fix a sucker onto an arm, and then could pull it free. It was Anna's call, her expertise, and frankly Devilly felt no urge to assist.

Devilly drifted around to the sofa where only a few hours before she had been sitting as Bling explained his demands. The glass-topped table on which she had spread the contract before signing was still in its place in front of the porthole window, and beside it was stack of freshly printed *Serial Suckers*—crisp and neat they looked, and she could imagine the delicious smell of newly printed plastic if she cracked a cover. No point in rewriting now to promote the image and reputation of Bling, but at least she would have to change the names to avoid any problems with his estate. The books would have to go back to the printers, although she doubted if they would accept "printing error" as a reason for their return. It would be worth a try, though, and she was determined to get to the bottom of the mystery of why the name of her character had been changed.

To distract herself from the proceedings,

Devilly let the tips of a couple of her tentacles absentmindedly rummage down the crack at the back of the sofa. One never knew. But no luck: there were no coins—only a pencil stub, a rubber band and an item that puzzled her when she first pulled it out. It was, she suddenly realized, another screw cap. She fingered it with her tentacle tip, marveling once again at the ingenuity of the Arboreals—the groove that spiraled around the metal cap was soothing to the touch. Devilly slipped the bottle cap into her mantle, together with the cap that Anna had just unscrewed from the Jeroboam. It was slightly smaller in diameter, but both could make satisfactory coral planters for her garden back in Nether Vortex. She would pack them carefully in her bags when she got back to the room.

Anna gave a triumphant exclamation, and Devilly assumed that she had succeeded in extracting Sir Callas and the mysterious third party. She glanced in the bedroom: there was Bling, trying to ascend to the ceiling but being held down by Roger, while his companion in death floated beside him, stiff as a brush.

Suddenly, Mrs. Blackpen burst into the suite. She thrust past Constable Grunion—somewhat recovered and intent on securing the perimeter—to get a glimpse of the Jeroboam.

"Oh my," she exclaimed. "How dreadful, poor Sir Callas, with that hussy too, and in our Jeroboam! Well, I never... Here, let me just..."

Mrs. Blackpen pulled a polaroid camera from the voluminous recesses of her mantle and, before anyone could stop her, took a picture. Devilly had no doubt that it would soon appear in one of the Gyre scandal sheets under a headline like *Horror at Bottlings*.

"That hussy, Mrs. Blackpen?" Devilly asked. "Do you know who Bling was having an affair with?"

"Oh, no, I'm not one to gossip. What a guest does is their own business, provided they pay for a double. Sir Callas always paid for a double. So, I say, live and let live, if they don't mess the sheets."

"That hussy?"

"Well, I'm not telling what everyone knows

anyway. It's not as though it was a secret. And Sir Callas being such a generous man with his tips. She is that Professor's so-called research assistant. I know what kind of research she was up to, if you know what I mean."

"You mean that you think he was sleeping with Serpie Argo?"

"Once a hussy, always a hussy, I always say. Her and her tattoos."

"Tattoos?"

"Yes, another of those 'One in a Thousand' people."

Devilly wondered how Anna would react; she wasn't about to tell her—by the time Anna extracted the girl from the bottle the tattoo would have faded. Anna seemed upset enough by this One in a Thousand business.

Mrs. Blackpen fussed about the room for a few minutes, sniffing at the mess. She patted the sofa cushions, arranging them to her satisfaction, and then excused herself, claiming she could not stand the sight of blood. Devilly looked quickly around for Professor van Oesterhuis, but he too had disappeared.

# Chapter 20

THE THUDDING APPROACH of a kelpchopper, as it beat its way towards a berth in the flooded campground behind the Inn, alerted everyone to the imminent arrival of the murder squad from Centro Police Headquarters.

In the Jeroboam Suite, Anna Teuthis paused in her dissection.

"Looks like the cavalry has arrived, Constable Grunion."

Anna had two bodies tethered to the floor: Bling—fat and bloated—and the thin waif-like remains of Serpie Argo. The former flopped in an unpleasant manner while Serpie seemed much too stiff, as if paralyzed. Not rigor, thought Devilly: this is the result of kissing of a blue-ring.

Devilly, holding down Bling at Anna's insistence, saw that the prospect of Inspector Hardcrabbie's wrath made Grunion turn a ghostly pale. She suspected that the officer had flouted almost every procedure for a scene of crime, and to top it all, here he was holding down the remaining arms of Bling for the doctor's knife. He would be caught red-handed in a dereliction of duty. Or green-handed—she corrected herself—as the verdant stain streamed from Anna's cut.

At least, Devilly reflected, Roger Seethe-Mantle had succeeded in flushing the onlookers from the Jeroboam suite, having rediscovered his parade-ground voice.

"Out, everyone," he had ordered. "Reconvene in the lounge at 1400 hours. You too, Margo." Even the green gelatinous blob that had followed the Ramblers from the Public disentangled to reveal two hunt protesters.

"Okay, Man," said one, "keep your ink in."

"This is so cool," said the other, and they both trailed Margo out into the tunnel.

✧　✧　✧

FIVE MINUTES LATER, Devilly heard Roger returning, apparently guiding the new arrivals to the Jeroboam Suite.

"I'm a military man myself, Inspector," she heard him say, just before they turned into the room. "I've tried to keep the civilians calm, but . . ."

Devilly look up from holding down Bling—whose bloated body free of restraint threatened to float away. In the entrance to the suite were two plain clothes octopolice, one small and angry, the other hulking. Roger was grinning inanely between them.

"This is Inspector Duncan Hardcrabbie," offered Roger, "and . . . ?"

"Sergeant Pulper," said the larger.

"What eejit is responsible for this?" growled the Inspector.

Anna Teuthis stopped an incision she was on the point of making, and approached Hardcrabbie, tentacle reaching out in greeting.

"I'm Dr. Teuthis. I'm a pathologist from Centro and have—as you can see—begun the post-mortem in the presence of Constable Grunion and my friend, who is also experienced in murder. I considered it vital to get started as soon as possible. The rate of decomposition, you know . . ."

"Bosh," said Hardcrabbie. "Ye canna do this. You're a suspect."

"No, I don't think you heard me, I am the resident pathologist at the central morgue."

"And ye can put down that scalpel. Sergeant, get these folk away from the scene. How many bodies?"

"Three," muttered Anna.

"Three! I heard one."

"No, that one is upstairs in the freezer. These are two fresh ones."

"What a muckle of eejits. Who are these then? Do they have names?"

"The blue-ring is Callas Bling," interjected Devilly. "And the small one is Serpitula Argo, a friend."

"Sir Callas Bling, eh? So, we are too late. And who the hell are you?"

"I'm Devilly Peen"

A smile like a gaping clam spread across Hardcrabbie's face. He looked at Sergeant Pulper and nodded.

"We have been looking for you, Ms. Peen. Right across the Gyre. I am so glad to meet you at last."

Devilly had a sinking feeling. "Whatever for? Has something happened in Nether Vortex? Has there been a burglary at Rose Grottage?"

"Not at all. I am arresting you for conspiracy to murder one Ordo Whitecuttle, as you describe in your book *Pretty in Gelatin*, and Sir Callas Bling, first victim in *Serial Suckers*. We are also investigating some—how many Pulper?—aye, forty-three other potential murders. Now it seems we can add a Patron of the Arts and a major contributor to the police widows and orphans fund to your list."

# Chapter 21

WHAT A MESS, thought Devilly, as she sat at a table in the public bar, tethered to the bench by zip ties. Sergeant Pulper sat opposite her, under instructions from Inspector Hardcrabbie not to let her out of his sight, and to allow no contact with the other guests. The Inspector would be interviewing "that barrel of ninnies" in the Lounge and had sent Grunion outside to look for clues—mainly, Devilly thought, to keep that embarrassment to the force out of the way.

The only upside from Devilly's viewpoint was that the bar was empty except for the Sergeant. She could sit in silence and think.

She had been searched of course. As the officers confiscated the contents of her poison sack, she realized—as she heard them exclaim with each new find—that this did not look good. Most damning, however, were the metal screw tops that she had thought perfect for seeding coral polyps.

Hardcrabbie had pounced on them.

"Sergeant, away you and see if one of these fits yon Jeroboam."

Pulper had returned minutes later to confirm that yes, the wider bottle top matched the Jeroboam.

"It is a perfect seal, sir. Whoever screwed this on must have known those inside would suffocate."

"Aye, means and opportunity, Sergeant. As for motive, what drives a sociopath like her will be up to the head doctors."

Devilly had protested: she had just found one of the tops down the back of the sofa and Dr. Teuthis had handed her the other; Sir Callas himself had asked her to rewrite *Serial Suckers* to change the victim and make him into a successful amateur detective in the place of Daisy Cuttle. She had a contract! As for the collection of poisons, it was just a hobby and . . ."

"Aye, a likely story. Ye took a contract all right." retorted Hardcrabbie. "I ken ye creative types—you commit murder over punctuation. Now, just bide here until I am ready to take you back to Centro. Keep a good watch on her, Sergeant, while I finish up in the Lounge."

So Devilly sat. What was it like in prison? Would she share a cell with some vastly overweight cuttle who masturbated? Would there be nothing to read? With that thought, her eyes wandered to a magazine that someone had left on the bench beside her. She picked it up—a recent edition of PlayFish. It was quite an interesting magazine provided one ignored the more salacious articles and the excess of advertising. There were always one or two serious articles worth reading: she had contributed a short piece herself—years ago—on the commoner species of venomous cone shells to be encountered around the Gyre.

Devilly flipped through the pages—past the promotional articles for exotic fishing holidays, past advice on technique for capturing lionfish without impaling oneself; she glanced briefly at a promotion for an all-inclusive resort on *Isla Florida*—as if she would try that again! She stopped dead, however, when the title of a long article caught her eye—*The Professor and Me* by Serpie Argo.

Sex and academic malpractice at Centro University, she read: how Professor "X" fakes his research, fails to credit the work of his research assistants, and makes unwelcome advances. Devilly felt her hearts race; things began to click into place. No prize for guessing "X" was a certain van Oesterhuis! So Serpie Argo had the dirt on the Professor, did she?

The taste—that was it!—the taste of the water when she had first entered the Jeroboam Suite. She had not placed it at the time—it was very faint—and then Roger had flung open the porthole. But now she was sure—there had been the hint of Black Slug, the most potent toxin of the highly toxic nudibranch clan. She had read that this particular venom caused immediate paralysis in its victims, and death usually followed from asphyxiation. The effects—she suddenly realized—were indistinguishable from that of tetradotoxin, the blue-ring venom.

The specimen van Oesterhuis had misidentified as *versicolor* on the day after the storm was of the family of the black slugs. Supposing, just supposing van Oesterhuis had decided to rid himself of his awkward research assistant? A black slug would come in handy. If only she could talk to Anna.

"Could I possibly get a message to Dr. Teuthis, Sergeant? It is very important."

Sergeant Pulper, sitting opposite Devilly, was watching the big screen on the far wall of the Public. From what she could tell, a repeat episode of Go-Fish! was showing, its awful host mouthing silently, since the sound was off.

"Sergeant?"

"What?"

"Please ask Dr. Teuthis to check whether there is a trace of black slug in the juices of Bling and Serpie Argo. It is a species of nudibranch."

"Nude what?" Pulper took his notebook from his mantle. "How do you spell that?"

# Chapter 22

AFTER WHAT SEEMED an age sitting in the Public Bar with Sergeant Pulper, Devilly suddenly heard the voice of Mr. Blackpen. He was complaining loudly.

"It's the Humboldts, Inspector, I tell you. Them squid are destroying my business!"

"Ach, Blackpen, hush yersel'. The doctor says they are knife wounds, not slashes from squid claws. Van Oesterhuis was knifed to death."

The weed curtain was violently brushed aside, and Inspector Hardcrabbie entered the bar, the landlord fast on his heels.

"Sir?" asked Pulper.

"Another one, Sergeant. Best get yer notebook out: I'm losing count here." He sat down in front of Devilly, tentacles coiled like fists and forehead a fierce crimson. "Now, Ms. Peen, what do you know about a fella called van

Oesterhuis?"

"X"

"What do ye mean 'X'? Talk sense woman."

"He is the unknown quantity! Am I to understand that the Professor is dead?"

"Aye, Grunion found him bobbing in the Blue Lagoon, being attended to by hungry garbage fish; the man seems to have a talent for stumbling on corpses. Yon Dr. Teuthis says he couldn't have been there for more that an hour or the body would have been entirely consumed."

"Well, Inspector, in that case, I have Sergeant Pulper here for an alibi. I didn't slip out to commit murder, did I Sergeant? And then return to reattach these zip ties?" Devilly looked meaningfully at the restraints. "I think you can remove these. I promise not to swim for it. Then I will explain about 'X'."

But Inspector Hardcrabbie—as emerged when Devilly pointed out Serpie Argo's article—had little time for academic scandals.

"But this is the same Serpitula Argo as the dead young woman in the Jeroboam!" insisted Devilly.

"Pure coincidence."

"My theory," began Devilly, "is that . . ."

But Hardcrabbie dealt in facts not—as he called it—"airy faerie speculation."

"You're nae arrested for the murder of van Oesterhuis, woman."

Hardcrabbie turned to his inferior. "Have ye located Sir Callas Bling's valet? I want a wee word with that sushi chef."

"No, sir. He seems to have disappeared."

"Well, Ms. Peen. Would ye know where he might be? Or, have ye got another corpse stashed away somewhere?"

"Ahem?"

Hardcrabbie turned towards the interruption. Mr. Blackpen—who had retreated behind the bar in a sulk and had been polishing the bar top with intent—was holding out a telephone receiver to the inspector.

"A call for you, Hardcrabbie."

"Get Grunion to start a search, Sergeant. I have nae doubt he will trip over the body if it is out there." The Inspector grabbed the receiver from Blackpen. "Yes?"

It is strange, thought Devilly, how colour

betrays an octopod's emotions: the sunset red—Hardcrabbie's normal colour—paled to that of a bilious sun seen through a veil of cloud. It was a one-way conversation since the officer, after an initial splutter, had ceased to speak.

✧   ✧   ✧

RELIEF FLOODED THROUGH her when Devilly recognized her nephew's voice. Embarrassingly for Hardcrabbie, the person at the other end of the phone was speaking loudly enough for everyone in the bar to overhear, and Chief Inspector Moray's tone to his subordinate was scathing.

Had Hardcrabbie read the Devilly Peen novels he had confiscated? No? Did Hardcrabbie not realize that prolific authors like Devilly Peen often used Artificial Intelligence? He didn't? Had Hardcrabbie spoken with Anenome, Devilly's secretary? He hadn't?

Despite being tethered to the table, Devilly managed to edge closer.

If he had, continued the Chief Inspector,

Hardcrabbie might have learned that his Aunt used WordScribblerXT to edit her employer's manuscripts directly from her tapes. Word-ScribblerXT was an editing bot based on a remote server. If the Inspector had done his homework, he would have learned the XT had form for hallucinating and was the object of a separate enquiry by Centro's cyber-crime squad. In this case the bot must have inserted what it regarded as more suitable victims into Devilly's novels: in *Serial Suckers*, for instance, the prominent Sir Callas Bling—wealthy and doubtless guilty of countless white-collar crimes—must have seemed a worthier victim than Slipper Batch, petty thief and a complete *inconnu*. So, should you wish to arrest a cloud, Hardcrabbie, be my guest. But enjoy the rest of your career directing turd in a sewage lagoon. Now, release my aunt!

"Aye, Chief. Immediately."

Hardcrabbie slammed the telephone down on the bar.

"Something to drink, Inspector?" Blackpen chuckled, his good humour regained.

"Gimme a whisky. Make it a double."

The Inspector looked hard at Devilly, before draining the glass with one convulsion. He cut Devilly free of the zip ties muttering something in gaelic that Devilly chose to take as an apology.

"No harm done, Inspector," said Devilly graciously. "Now perhaps I can return to the Lounge and rejoin my friends."

A grinning Blackpen held back the curtain as Devilly led Hardcrabbie and Pulper up through the tunnel to *Bubbles*. Inside the Lounge were gathered all the remaining guests, their numbers diminished by murderous attrition. All looked up hopefully as they entered.

"Devilly!" cried Anna. "They've let you go? Thank Goodness! I managed to get hold of your nephew at headquarters: he was furious—something about compromising an investigation. Did he reach you, Inspector?"

"Aye," replied Hardcrabbie. "He did that."

✧　✧　✧

"OH, MY DEAR, how dreadful, I never heard the

like." Mrs. Blackpen emerging from the kitchen with a plate piled high with crabmeat sandwiches caught sight of Devilly. "A guest of ours falsely arrested so Mr. Blackpen says"—she glowered at the police officers—"tied up in the Public Bar, and you being a lady, well I never. And me completely out of Tupperware what the doctor needs for her bodies."

"I'm quite all right, Mrs. Blackpen . . ."

"And that Mrs. Mantle here was just saying that she wasn't a bit surprised, and Mr. McKraken and Mr. Mantle almost coming to blows, and then Tom Grunion finding that poor Professor Oesterhuis, I just thought *sandwiches*. And Blackpen is offering a round on the house—just one mind. Blackpen! Bring the tea!"

✧  ✧  ✧

GRATEFULLY ACCEPTING A sachet of the house brew—made palatable with two lumps—Devilly was amused to watch the Inspector attempt to regain his dignity. He was, after all, the senior officer on a scene with multiple suspicious deaths. Hardcrabbie coughed loudly.

"If you would all sit yerselves and stop floating about." The sudden swirl of arms and tentacles that Devilly's reappearance had excited slowly subsided. "Aye, that's better. Now, Doctor, my Chief asked if you would give your professional opinion on the multiple deaths we have here."

Anna ignored the Inspector and spoke directly to Devilly. She gestured to wards the four plastic boxes stacked in the corner of Lounge.

"Those contain the remains of Tenta, Bling, Argo and van Oesterhuis, in order of decease. I've just had a look at van Oesterhuis after Grunion hauled him in from the beach. He was slashed to death with a special kind of knife, just like Tenta. The wounds are a very good imitation of those I would normally attribute to Humboldt Squid. Did you know Cally Bling's valet has disappeared?"

"Bling said his man was an artist with a knife."

"You think he is guilty?"

"Yes, in part."

"What do you mean 'in part'?"

"You didn't test Bling and Argo for Black Slug, did you Anna?"

Devilly suddenly felt everyone watching her. They were not seeing her, she suddenly realized; they were looking at Daisy Cuttle, her fictional detective. They were waiting for the denouement.

"I was just asking myself," continued Devilly, after seeing Anna shake her head, "that perhaps we have it all back to front."

"You mean the deaths of Bling and Argo, and of Tenta and now the Professor, by suffocation and by knife?" asked Anna.

"Aye, different *modi operandi*; two different killers," interjected Inspector Hardcrabbie.

"Yes, Inspector, I believe you are correct. The deaths are linked, and I think I understand why. For me, motive has been more of a puzzle than means. Why would anyone want to murder Serpie Argo, on the one hand, yet just about all gathered here at *Bubblings* might have reason to dispose of Bling."

"Here, hold on a minute!" exclaimed Roger.

"We've interviewed everyone," objected the Inspector. "They all have alibis: no one was near the Jeroboam Suite."

"You can't have interviewed van Oesterhuis. He was already dead on the beach."

"You mean, you think he murdered Bling, and was then murdered himself?"

"Yes, and he used a nudibranch toxin from a black slug to do it. A tetradotoxin, as I'm sure you know, Inspector, causes the same symptoms as the bite of a blue-ring. But that is not my point. His target was Serpie Argo. She was about to expose his academic cheating and ruin his career. Maybe she was blackmailing him."

"So, according to you, Bling was not the intended victim?"

"Sir Callas Bling was a notorious philanderer. He had already seduced every young octo on the premises, and van Oesterhuis realized that he could implicate Bling by making Argo's murder look like a typical blue-ring date gone wrong. They often do; the police files must be full of such accidental deaths. But Bling was by-catch; the Professor wanted to rid himself of his dangerous research assistant: opportunity presented itself, and he took it."

Roger was squirming with impatience.

"But, if that's the case, there is another murderer out there. Who killed the Professor?"

"Now, I'm afraid I must speculate. Bling relied on the loyalty of his valet and sushi chef to clean up the unfortunate aftermaths of his affairs. Young Tenta was a sad example, and there may have been many others over the years, all conveniently blamed on the Humboldt Squid. Van Oesterhuis killed his master, and Tako-san exacted revenge: his last duty to his employer. From his point of view, it was the honourable thing to do."

Anna looked doubtful.

"That's very clever, Devilly. But Bling and Argo were suffocated, and we found them together in the Jeroboam."

"Serpie was stiff and paralyzed, if I recall, but Bling was flaccid. I think Serpie was paralysed by van Oesterhuis, and inserted into the bottle beside Bling who was already dead by suffocation."

"The ship-in-a-bottle technique. How clever. Insert the stiff body of Argo, and as the poison wore off, it would relax and expand to fill the bottle with Bling."

"Exactly."

# Chapter 23

"So can we all go home, now that my friend Devilly has solved your case for you?"

Margo had learned from Mr. Blackpen that municipal workers had successfully lassoed *Bottlings* and reconnected it to the Gyre; the way to the village of Crabster and the road back to Nether Vortex were open again. She had Inspector Hardcrabbie backed into a corner by Reception and was using the voice Devilly had last heard organizing the Nether Vortex Open Day when many of the exhibitors had simply not read the rules.

"Aye, ye can all go." The search for Bling's valet had been called off, and the Inspector and Sergeant Pulper were preparing to leave. Devilly could hear the Kelpchopper reving up behind the Inn. "Constable Grunion will be remaining here until we can transfer the remains to Centro."

Mrs. Blackpen had insisted the Grunion stay. Because "her Tom" would make sure the police returned her Tupperware boxes once they had been emptied and "thoroughly cleaned, mind!"

It was far too late to drive home that night.

"In that case, why don't you come and see my Grottage," said Rory McKraken to Margo. "It is only a short drive up the Arm."

"What a wonderful idea!"

"I might as well come along too," said Roger gloomily. "We can take the SeaRover."

Which left the prospect of herself and Anna alone at the Inn, and finally able to relax. Bliss. But for the moment, Anna was in the lounge busy writing up her official reports—Devilly had a couple of hours to herself.

She would call Bling's Books in Centro. It was only fair: she felt guilty that her silly mistake had disrupted Leo's plans for a book launch. He knew he must be out of pocket for advertising, her fans disappointed. She would remedy that as soon as possible. She went to the pay phone behind Reception.

She knew she had the number somewhere, and as she searched, her eyes ran over the numerous business cards that had been tucked into the crack between the wall and the phone: numbers for a local taxi, a fish and chip in Crabster, a local hairdresser.

Why was this card so familiar? She retrieved it with a sucker and read: *One in a Thousand*. It carried the same logo as the tattoos on Tenta and Serpie Argo! Beneath the title in small letters the card proclaimed: "No more staffing problems—call *One in a Thousand* for all your staffing needs—maids, gardeners, cooks, waiters, research assistants."

Poor Anna. If only she would wear her reading glasses, she would have avoided all that worry about the choice she had made so many years ago about her eggs. The threats Anna complained of receiving through her bottle mail were merely advertising home help: no one was persecuting her. It was nothing personal. Devilly chuckled. Would she tell Anna? Of course she would!

Devilly found the number she was looking for and dialed Bling's Books.

"Hello, Leo? I just wanted to say how sorry I am about your uncle."

"Yeah, I guess. The old bastard had it coming."

"And to let you know I am sending *Serial Suckers* for reprint. So, in about two weeks I should be free for a book signing."

"You are not planning to be arrested again, then?"

"Leo, notoriety has its own cachet. If I were you, I would order a lot more of my books."

The connection was abruptly terminated. Probably a technical fault, thought Devilly. Leo Bling would never cut her.

✦　✦　✦

DRIFTING BACK TO the Annex and *Beaujolais*, Devilly noticed that the Blue Lagoon was now open to guests. Why not?—it had been a while since she had enjoyed a decent swim. Presumably it had been dragged of all remaining bodies.

Barely bothering to change her colours for something more suitable, she swam to the middle of the pool, and allowed herself to sink downwards. The passing walls of the pool were smeared with a pale gesso, giving a smooth finish on which someone had painted imagined scenes of coral reefs. Crude and nothing like the original, thought Devilly. At the very bottom of the pool was a shut clam, an emergency exit. Curious, Devilly pushed down the locking bar. The clam swung open, and she found herself hovering above the infinity of the ocean depths.

The coolness of the water was striking, a pleasant contrast with the over-warm and stuffy aquaclimate of the Inn. (No matter which knob Devilly had tried, she could not seem to vary the temperature in her room.) Now, this refreshing draft of the real ocean was most welcome. Devilly was on a high: she had bested the police by solving four murders; her reputation as a detective had appreciated enormously, and she had learned some useful facts about her fellow Nether Vortex Ramblers for future reference. She was feeling adventurous, perhaps a little reckless: she would swim down into open water—not too far and staying close to the bottom keel of the Inn.

It was delightful to float suspended in the void, and a great relief to stretch her arms to their full extent after being confined in the Inn or curled up in her bottle. She expelled a great jet and let herself glide backwards, eight arms trailing. It was so relaxing! Above, sunlight filtering through the mash of plastic created a flickering kaleidoscope of yellows and greens and blues. Below, there was only the ever-deepening ultramarine of increasing depth, shading to abyssal black. She gently contracted again—a mere puff from her siphon—and drifted on beneath the keel of plastic. What an abundance of colonizing marine life!—the drooping fruit of barnacles, clusters of feather worms contracting into their tubes as she passed, the contortions of brittle stars in their ballet practice, groping anemones; even a few small corals had decided to make this foreign substrate home.

She reached the edge of the raft and glided along the ragged margin scattering schools of tiny fish. Now, all she could see overhead was the mirrored oval of the sky at the ocean surface, the light slanting down, unrefracted by garbage, dappling back and forth with the gentle swell. It was quite mesmerizing.

A sibilant whistle brought her up short, her arms bunched defensively. She was suddenly acutely aware of her vulnerability, suspended in mid-water. Wild swimming does not come naturally to octopods, and she looked around with growing alarm for something to cling to, something to model for camouflage. The raft was by now a dim shadow at the edge of sight, around her the blue stretched to infinity.

Another whistle sounded behind her, and she spun about ready to empty her ink sack—something she hadn't done for ages. There, hovering mere metres away was a Humboldt Squid. It was side on to her, its long torpedo of a body a brilliant scarlet. At the business end, horridly hooked tentacles flared around a viciously curved beak. One of its enormous round eyes assessed her—Devilly assumed as to her edibility.

A cloud of ink, but how should she shape it? What did Humboldts eat anyway? Perhaps if she shot ink in the shape of a fish, that would be enough to distract it?

The whistling lowered in pitch. As it tailed off into a sort of burble, she began to imagine that she was hearing some kind of language. Talk to it, that was it! Be firm. Do not, do not turn and swim for it!

"Is Madam lost, by any chance?" The accent was strange, but it was definitely Octo, the *lingua franca* of the ocean. The Humboldt spoke Octo!

"Well! What a fright you gave me!"

"My dear lady, let me put your mind at rest. Humboldts do not eat octopods out of season. We have a Treaty."

This was news to Devilly, but living in Nether Vortex, she paid little attention to Aboriginal Affairs. She vaguely knew that the vast plastic agglomeration that constituted the Gyre spread over waters that certain indigenous species regarded as their tribal seas, but surely all that was settled generations ago. Octopods came from a different planet, and the natives had surely benefited from Octo technology that was far in advance of anything on this world. And what with intermarriage and a liberal government, relations between octos and the native squid had never seemed so tranquil.

"There are exceptions, of course. But, happily for you, our lunar excesses are over for this month. Some of the younger spirits get a little wild, as you will understand, but simple precautions should keep you safe."

Such precautions including a large ink gun, and a handy selection of neurotoxins, thought Devilly.

"How interesting. I am grateful to you, Mr. . . . .er?"

"I regret our names are untranslatable into your tongue. You would hear it as a bubbling scream. Mine is quite alarming, I'm told."

"I see." Devilly had a quick look around. She now had no idea in which direction lay safety; the currents below the raft must have been stronger than she thought. She was now suspended in a featureless void with an enormous predatory squid hovering a mere tentacle strike away. It was time to assert herself with this squid. "Perhaps you would be so good as to direct me back to the Inn? I'm staying at

*Bottlings.*"

"Of course. You must be a guest of the Blackpens. We have what you might call a working relationship: they don't interfere with our fish quota, and we don't interfere with their guests."

"Oh, and did you know Sir Callas Bling?"

"Indeed. We heard he had died. He styled himself Master of Squid, but it was just a show to impress the investors. He may have been a Master of Real Estate and a power in Centro, but out here he was just another rich cottager. I have to say he paid well, though, for us to look after things in his absence. We didn't mind giving him and his city cronies rides when we corralled a shoal of fish. It was quite funny reenacting a hunt. And, if a porpoise ever dares to show its nasty snout in our waters, we would know what to do about it. But they are seldom so stupid," concluded the Humboldt, wistfully.

"Perhaps I should be getting back?" said Devilly, who was beginning to miss the comforting intimacy of *Bottlings*, despite Mrs. Blackpen's unfortunate predilection for pastel decor. Collapsing into a comfortable clam in the lounge, buried in bubble wrap and safe from the pelagic predators of the open ocean suddenly seemed attractive to Devilly.

"Certainly, in due course. But it is nearly time for our communal supper. We Humboldts eat together, and one must be there on time because the food seldom lasts long. You should really learn about the real Humboldt. We wish to be portrayed in a better light in your next book."

Devilly quailed at thought of a swarm of Humboldt Squid devouring their prey.

"I think I must be going . . ."

"I daresay you are getting tired of Mrs. Blackpen's crab-in-a-basket? You should try some real country food."

"Really, I . . ."

"Let me invite you to dinner, Ms. Peen. To-night, we have a special treat."

"Tempting, but I must decline . . ."

"We are having Tako."

The End

# Other titles by E.K. Wicher in the Devilly Peen murder mystery series...

The Gyre

Thank Goodness for Poisonous Snails

Ekwicher.com